LAURA WOOD

VOTE
FOR Effie
★ ★ ★ ★ ★

Blue Peter
BOOK AWARDS 2020
SHORTLIST

ILLUSTRATED BY MIRELLE ORTEGA

SCHOLASTIC

ALSO BY
Laura Wood:

Poppy Pym and the Pharaoh's Curse
Poppy Pym and the Double Jinx
Poppy Pym and the Smuggler's Secret
Poppy Pym and the Beastly Blizzard

Effie the Rebel

For everyone who marched, with love and gratitude.

PART ONE

The Candidate

CHAPTER *One*

"Yoo . . . fee . . . mee . . . a Kostas?" the teacher's voice rings out uncertainly.

A few snickers rattle around the room, but I paste on a bright smile.

"Here, miss," I say. "But you can call me Effie." It's the third time I've had to say that today. That's one of the problems with starting at a new school if you have an unusual name – the register can be a bit of an ordeal for you *and* your teacher. Especially if you're stuck with a name like Euphemia. (It's actually pronounced "Yoo-fem-ia", by the way.)

"It means well-spoken," I add, and the teacher, who was about to move on to the next name on her list, falters.

"I'm sorry?" She looks over at me, and there are more muffled laughs from my fellow students.

I push back my frizz of dark hair, which seems to be growing bigger and bigger as the day goes on. "My name," I say. "It's from the Greek for well-spoken, or good speaker." I like to try and get this fact in whenever my full name comes up. I don't really like it very much, to be honest, but it is important to try and make lemonade out of lemons. Being saddled with a name like Euphemia is a pretty sour lemon to suck on, but at least I approve strongly of the meaning behind it.

"My dad chose it," I continue, though the teacher is still looking a little blank. Perhaps she needs a cup of coffee? (I've actually got into coffee lately. Well ... I drank a vanilla latte with extra sugar and whipped cream on Saturday and the effects were most invigorating. Mum said my eyes were a bit wild-looking and that she thought in future I should stick to decaf, but I got ever such a lot of unpacking done, and I sorted all my books – by genre (and alphabetically, of course, I'm not an animal) – ready for shelving once Dad helps me to put all my new bookcases together.

I was quite keen to tackle this myself as I'm all for female empowerment, but Dad said he thought that my female empowerment should come without its own power tools until I'm at least sixteen, and even though I told him that response was sexist nonsense I have to admit that he might have a point after that tiny little incident with the water pipe in our last house, but all of the furniture dried out fine so I don't really know what the fuss was about.)

Anyway, the point is that the teacher standing in front of me definitely looks in need of a caffeine boost. We're not that far into term but this lady looks completely frazzled already; her dark hair is falling out of the messy bun she has it stuffed into, and she keeps pushing a loose lock out of her eyes. Her hands are covered in ink stains and – now that I look at it a little more closely, the front of her shirt seems to have a big ink stain on it as well, one that she has tried to cover up with a brightly patterned scarf. I make all of these lightning-fast Sherlock-style deductions and something clicks as I realize that my new English teacher is having a Bad Day. I inject even more brightness into my voice as I continue to fill her in on the origins of my name.

"Dad said that my name fit me perfectly even as a baby," I beam, hoping that a little of my cheerfulness might rub off on to her. "Apparently I was quite noisy." I fold my hands in front of me on the desk, considering this. "But I do think it's important to make yourself heard, don't you, miss?" There are some more slightly nervous giggles from my classmates. As I look around I notice most of them look a bit dazed.

"Yes," the teacher agrees faintly. She is also looking, it has to be said, a little bewildered.

"I—" I begin, ready to deliver more interesting information, but I am cut off by the teacher, who slices her hand through the air in an impatient gesture.

"Yes, thank you, Effie," she says coolly. "Perhaps I had better share *my* name now. I am Miss Sardana." She pushes the stray bit of hair away from her face again in a frustrated motion. "I was going to wait until the end of the register to have you introduce yourself, but as you seem to have started that ball rolling, perhaps you'd like to do it now?"

This is fine with me. I am not exactly what my mum calls a "shrinking violet". I get to my feet, and my chair makes a little squeaking sound as I push it backwards. I smooth my hands over my school skirt, annoyed again that I don't have the option to wear trousers like the boys do if I am in the mood (what is this, Victorian times?!).

"Well, my name's Effie," I say, using my best public speaking voice, which is good and loud. "I just moved here last week, which is why I'm a bit late starting school. I have a little sister called Lil. She's eight, so she's not at secondary school yet. My dad is a copy editor and he works from home so that he can look after us. My mum is a lecturer and she's doing research on a poet from the thirteenth century who no one has ever heard of, but that will all change when she's finished her book. That's why we moved here," I add. "Because she got a new job at the university."

I'm speaking quickly, because even when you're quite a confident person, it's often difficult to stand in front of a group of strangers and talk. I take a deep breath. "I play the violin . . . but not very well," I add hastily, because I really do think that honesty is the best policy. "I'm trying to convince my dad to let me have a dog. I would call it Emmeline Pankhurst, even if it was a boy dog. I'm a feminist and musical theatre enthusiast." I tip my head thoughtfully to one side, trying to work out if I've forgotten anything. "Ah –" I lift my finger "– and my favourite colour is green or sometimes purple."

If anything, Miss Sardana looks even wearier now. "Thank you, Effie," she murmurs as I sit back down.

"Oh!" I leap to my feet. "And I forgot to say, miss. I think anyone should have a choice to wear trousers OR a skirt to school if they want. This school uniform policy is from the dark ages." I glance around at my fellow pupils, expecting their enthusiastic support, but most of them aren't even looking at me, and those who are look vaguely startled by my outburst.

"That is not really an appropriate subject for our English lesson," Miss Sardana sighs. "Let's not get distracted. Please sit down quietly now so that we can get on."

"But, miss," I persist. "Someone should do something about it!"

"Well, that is something for you to take up with

the student council, Effie, now *please, sit down.*" I do so, reluctantly, as the rest of the class bursts into muted chatter.

The giggling and whispering continue and so Miss Sardana lifts her voice with a visible effort, moving on with the register and then beginning to talk about *A Midsummer Night's Dream*, which is the play the class have been studying since the start of term. I scribble a lot of notes, pulling out all of my different coloured highlighters and sharpening my pencils, surreptitiously breathing in the woody pencil-sharpening smell. I love the start of the school year.

Not that it's exactly been easy this time. Today is my first day at Highworth Grange secondary school and I'm already a whole month behind everyone else. I don't know anybody, and the school is absolutely massive. It's one of those buildings that's had loads of bits added on to it over the last hundred years or so and none of the room numbers make any sort of logical sense, and some of them have random letters in front so sometimes you think you've reached the top of a staircase and then there's another sort of extra bit that takes you by surprise. Still, it's important to remain positive. I am trying very hard to think of the move as a new opportunity, and ignoring the pang of homesickness that I feel when I think of my old familiar house and my old familiar school.

I pull a map from my pocket and have a quick look at it, noting Miss Sardana's name in the little square that represents her classroom. The school secretary gave me a map when I came in for a tour a few weeks ago, but this is one that I drew myself while they were showing me around. It's a lot more accurate and has important notes about things that I noticed, like which are the cleanest toilets, and the shortest route to the canteen.

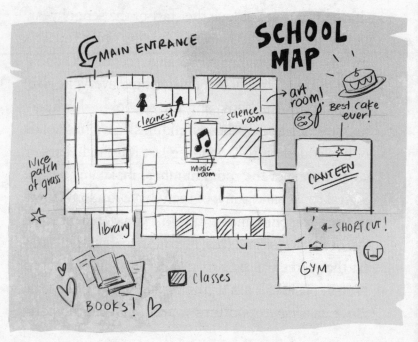

The bell rings to signal the end of the lesson and it's time for lunch. I join the stream of students in boxy black blazers headed towards the canteen, but unfortunately I can't join in any of the excited conversations that surround me. I do almost try with one group of girls from my English class, but they all have their backs firmly turned to me, like an impenetrable wall. I queue up, glancing longingly around for a friendly face, but none appear until the dinner lady smiles at me. I hand over my dinner money in exchange for a cheese and tomato sandwich and a packet of salt and vinegar crisps. I tried going vegan for a few weeks but my dad caught me gnawing on a lump of Edam in the middle of the night and insisted that I give it up so now I'm a vegetarian instead. Well, apart from chicken and bacon. And the occasional burger.

Looking around the crowded canteen, I feel an unfamiliar wave of panic rising inside me. I really don't know *anyone*. Not a single soul. And there aren't any encouraging, smiling faces looking in my direction, either. Instead everyone seems to be sitting in cosy, tight clusters, chatting and laughing quite happily. There's a table full of people who look like they're having a good time. They're shouting at each other and bursting into noisy explosions of laughter. There's a spare seat at their table on to which they've all dumped their coats and bags. *I should go and talk to them, I think. These could be my new best friends. There's no need to be nervous... I'm a nice person, anyone would be lucky to have me for a friend.* I can't help but notice that my own inner voice seems to be trying a bit too hard to convince me of this fact. I hover nearby and clear my throat. No one seems to notice, not even a flicker of attention comes my way. I clear my throat again, louder this time. Still nothing.

"Excuse me," I say finally, and my voice is a little croaky.

"Mmm." One of the girls slides her gaze over in my direction.

"I just wondered if I could sit here?" I say, pointing at the chair. I beam at her in my absolute friendliest manner.

"Sorry." The girl shrugs, not sounding particularly sorry at all. "That seat is taken." She turns immediately back to her neighbour and carries on her conversation as if I was never there at all.

I am left pink-cheeked and open-mouthed, gasping like a goldfish unceremoniously scooped out of its bowl. I look once more at the pile of bags and blazers that are apparently better company than me and I can feel tears burning at the backs of my eyes. *Don't you dare cry!* I tell myself sternly. Maybe it's not so bad, maybe they're just saving the seat for someone else who isn't there yet. There's no need to take it personally.

I blink hard and with a determined sniff, I sweep off, eventually perching on the end of a long table with a few empty seats. The boy nearest me doesn't even seem to notice. With a sigh I peel the cling film from around my sandwich and carefully remove the tomato slices. If I was in charge no one would be allowed to hog a whole chair like that. And no one would have to sit alone. I'd make sure that new students always had somewhere to sit and a friendly person to talk to. I munch forlornly on my sandwich.

Still, I think, recovering some of my brightness, it's only the first day. I'm sure I'll have made loads of friends by the end of the week. No need to panic.

CHAPTER *Two*

Absolutely no need to panic, I repeat to myself several times through the rest of the day as I battle increasingly violent waves of what can really only be described as panic. *It's fine. Everything is fine.* By the time the final bell rings my head is buzzing full of facts about Henry VIII and tricky long division and new faces and endless maze-like corridors. My total lack of friends has been weighing pretty heavily on my mind, I must admit, and so I have found it more difficult than usual to really concentrate on what my teachers were saying. Not ideal if you're already behind. Despite my usual cheeriness, by the time the last bell rings, I'm having to work hard not to let a general cloud of glumness engulf me.

It takes about fifteen minutes to walk to our new house from the school – sixteen if you're unlucky with the pedestrian crossing lights.

Our *new* house is actually a pretty *old* house. My mum and dad say that it's "bursting with character", which seems to be code for "none of the walls or floors are quite straight". It is nice though, our funny, wonky house. It is tall and thin and I have a whole attic room to myself, and I will get to choose how we decorate it once we've saved up a bit of money. It turns out moving house is an expensive business. The house has a little scruffy patch of garden out the front and a red door.

I am just pulling out my new set of keys when I hear someone talking.

"So you're the new neighbour then." A croaky voice reaches my ears.

The voice seems to be coming from the small hedge that separates our garden from next door, and for a second I stare at it in bemusement. My heart beats rapidly. Perhaps this is the start of a story where I get pulled into a magical hedge and I live among the tiny hedge people, helping them to battle injustices until I reluctantly agree to be their queen, ruling with wisdom and kindness for five hundred years.

"Why are you staring at my hedge like that?" the voice asks, and I realize with a mixture of sadness and relief (after all, I have a lot to do here and I haven't really got the time to become a hedge queen and to give my subjects the ruler they deserve) that the voice belongs to a woman.

I'm surprised I didn't notice her before, to be honest, but then her garden is so overgrown that she's pretty well hidden by weeds. She is sitting in a fold-out garden chair on her front step. The woman is quite small and old, maybe about eighty, but she has short, bright pink hair and she's reading a book.

"Hello," I call back, the key in my hand, as I stand poised to enter the house. Instead, I step over towards the (ordinary, non-magical) hedge because it's good to be polite. "Yes, I'm

one of your new neighbours," I shout. "My name's Effie."

"There's no need to shout," the woman grumbles. "I'm old, not deaf."

"Sorry," I say, lowering my voice to a more normal volume.

The woman looks me over for a moment, a thoughtful gleam in her pale blue eyes. It's not terribly warm out here, but she seems to have prepared for this by wrapping herself in a gigantic purple woollen poncho.

"Effie," she says finally. "Well, I'm Iris." She gives me another sharp look. "I hope you're not planning on having a lot of noisy parties? Loud music and hooligans arriving at all hours of the day and night?"

"No!" I splutter. "Of course not. I'm only twelve."

"Good," Iris grunts, although if I didn't know better, I'd think she was a bit disappointed.

"My sister sometimes turns the *Frozen* soundtrack up quite loud," I offer.

"Don't know what that is." Iris purses her lips. "And I don't think I want to."

"It's actually quite good," I say. "If you don't have to listen to it thirty-six times a day for months on end."

"Hmmm." Iris sniffs. "Well, in you go then, you'll be late for your tea."

We won't be having tea for hours yet but I don't want to be rude. "OK," I say instead. "It was nice to meet you."

Iris sniffs again, which I choose to translate as "the feeling is mutual".

I go back to the front door and turn the lock, tumbling into the warm hallway.

"Let it gooooooooooooooooo, let it goooooooooooooo," Lil's voice howls from up the stairs.

Dad appears from the kitchen, his dark hair rumpled and a pained expression on his face.

"I thought you hid her *Frozen* CD," I hiss.

"She found it," he replies mournfully. "Although I don't know how. I put it inside a bag of rice."

I shrug off my rucksack and my coat and blazer, hanging them on the hooks in the hallway, and follow my dad through to the kitchen. His laptop is open on the table, a stone-cold cup of tea beside it. The kitchen is a disaster area, full of half empty boxes and bags for life.

"How was school?" Dad asks as I sink into a chair.

"It was fine," I say as cheerfully as I can.

"Fine?" Dad repeats slowly, his eyes widening in concern. "Oh, no."

I suppose "fine" is a word I don't use that often. I'm

much fonder of "brilliant" or "amazing". Dad moves over the kitchen counter and plucks a pack of Penguin biscuits from the top of one of the bags, tearing the packet open with his teeth and chucking two right at me. He always knows how to cheer me up.

"I'll put the kettle on, shall I?" he says. "Then you can tell me all about it."

"OK," I say, summoning up a smile. "Sounds good."

After I've filled Dad in on the various injustices at my new school, like the restrictions on uniforms and the fact that no one seems very worried about welcoming new students, and helped him to unpack a couple more of the boxes, I head upstairs and stick my head around the door to Lil's room. She is lying on her bed dressed up as Olaf the snowman. We couldn't afford the proper Olaf the snowman costume so Dad made this one for her on his creaky old sewing machine and I think it's even better, apart from the slightly wonky nose, but Lil says that adds character.

"All right, Lil?" I ask.

She sits up and turns to me, a rather sinister grin spreading across her freckled face.

"Just in time for a duet!" she tinkles, heading for

the battered CD player that Dad gave her in what would prove to be the biggest mistake of his life.

"Can't stop," I say swiftly. "Homework, you know?" I spread my hands in front of me and arrange my face in an expression that I hope conveys plenty of regret.

Lil raises one eyebrow, a trick that she mastered surprisingly early in life, and one that she employs regularly to let her family know that she is wearied and unamused by them.

"How was the first day of school?" I ask.

Lil shrugs. "Good, I guess."

"Did you make any new friends?"

"Oh, yeah." Lil's attention returns to the CD player, and she holds her finger down on the skip button so that Idina Menzel sings out all squeaky and in reverse. Lil chuckles.

"So the other kids were nice?" I press.

Lil shrugs again, totally unconcerned. "They're OK. Treena, Kayla and Nadia all want to be my *best* friend. I told them I'd let them know my decision by the end of the week. We're doing auditions tomorrow."

"Right," I say, weakly. Of course Lil has everyone under her spell already.

"Did you make any new friends?" Lil asks.

"Oh, yeah, loads," I reply quickly, fixing a smile on my face.

"Never mind, Effie," Lil says pityingly. "It just takes a while for people to get to know you." She comes over and pats my arm reassuringly. "It'll be all right."

"Thanks," I manage to choke out. *Wonderful*, I think. *Even my eight-year-old sister thinks I'm a loser.*

"If you want, you can borrow my lucky purple glitter scrunchie," Lil calls after me as I leave the room. "That might help."

CHAPTER *Three*

A few days later I am starting to think the lucky scrunchie might be my only option. I'm still wandering the school halls like a complete loner, and it's really starting to get me down. *Where are all my fellow outcasts?* I wonder. Shouldn't there be loads of us, searching for each other? Am I looking in the wrong places? It's not even as if people are being mean to me ... they just don't seem to notice me at all, and in some ways that feels worse.

After grabbing my lunch I've been escaping to the quiet safety of the library. At least the books don't judge you or make you feel like a loser. The only bright spots in my days have been the particularly good slices of cake that the canteen have been serving. My old school didn't do puddings that were anywhere near as nice. That's something, I guess.

Last night when my mum came home from the university I have to confess I had a moment of weakness and cried a little bit into her shoulder. She was really nice about it, reassuring me that I'll get used to the new school and that of course I'll make friends, and that I'm brilliant and all that, but the point is she WOULD say that, wouldn't she? After all, she's my mother. She's genetically conditioned to like me so that she doesn't, like, accidentally wander off and leave me to be eaten by wolves or something. That's science.

It's not the people who are related to me who are the problem. Not to be dramatic or anything, but THEIR BLOOD RUNS IN MY VEINS. It's the people who don't share my DNA that don't seem terribly interested. I've tried striking up conversations with strangers, but mostly I just get funny looks and cold shoulders. I had a pretty promising exchange with a girl when I asked if I could borrow her Tipp-Ex (a cunning ruse, of course; as if I would come to school so unprepared), but after I complimented the viscosity of her chosen brand and there was a silence that lasted over ninety seconds (I counted in my head), that blossoming friendship fell by the wayside.

The school seems full of the usual cliques and gangs, and I've been observing them like I'm David Attenborough in the Sahara. *The alpha males make their presence known*, I narrate silently in my head as I watch a load of footballer lad types jostling and honking insults at each other in the corridor. They're getting ready to go and practise on the pristine AstroTurf. *Though physically strong, this particular baboon pack displays a worrying lack of intelligence. Communication seems to take place through a series of grunts and fart noises.* I pass by them and, as per usual, no one even seems to notice.

And here we see the birds of paradise. I stroll past a group of girls and boys who have somehow managed to make their school uniforms look cool. I recognize a couple of girls from my classes, including one called Katie who is flouting the rules by blowing bubbles with bright pink gum. *Their brightly coloured feathers and twittering music attracts plenty of attention.* This group is rowdy, yelling and laughing at each other. They slouch against the lockers and sprawl out on the floor like they own the place so that people have to step over them, which they do without comment.

"Would you mind moving your bag?" I ask a boy with curly golden hair. He is sitting with his back against the lockers and his legs spread out in front of him, taking up loads of space and not moving an inch when people have to keep scrambling around him and his backpack. I try to keep my voice polite but his whole attitude is annoying.

The boy squints up at me in surprise as though I am a piece of furniture that has suddenly started talking. "What?" He blinks.

"Your bag," I say slowly, pointing to the pristine designer backpack that is slumped a little way from him in the middle of the corridor. "Can you move it?"

The boy looks at it like he's never seen it before. "Can't you just step over it?" he asks, and then he turns to the person next to him and starts talking like I'm not there.

"Um, NO, ACTUALLY," I say loudly, disbelief fuelling my rage. "Your bag is blocking the hall and everyone else needs to be able to get past. You don't own the corridor, you know, it's really rude of you."

The boy rolls his eyes. "There's no need to shout," he mutters. "Is it really that big a deal? You're too lazy to walk around it?"

I gasp at this. Folding my arms tightly and trying

to keep my voice even, I channel Lil at her most withering. "I am not *shouting*," I bite off. "And the only lazy one here is you. Is it so difficult to locate your manners? Now, *please*. Move. Your. Bag." I glare at him.

With a sigh the boy leans over and grasps the strap on his backpack, giving it a half-hearted tug that moves it a couple of inches, just enough for me to get by. I sweep through, my nose in the air, trying to ignore the gaggle of students who have stopped to watch our conversation.

I suppose part of me was hoping for someone to start clapping slowly at the fearless way I was standing up for the masses. Then they would gradually be joined by others until a roar of applause and cheers would bounce off the walls and the crowd would start chanting my name, lifting me on to their shoulders and carrying me away on a tide of gratitude...

But I am sorely disappointed. Apart from a few mutterings and nervous looks in my direction, nothing else happens.

The confrontation leaves me shaking. As I trudge into the canteen for another lonely lunch, there is precisely one thing I'm looking forward to ... that slice of particularly good chocolate cake. Picking up my tray I hurry forward, noticing that the last piece is sitting temptingly on its little dish. I open my mouth to ask the dinner lady behind the counter for it when I am shoved slightly to one side and confronted by a large expanse of black blazer. It is the back of a boy who has just pushed in front of me in the queue, and he is ... the horror of it begins to dawn inside my foggy brain ... he is actually ordering the last piece of chocolate cake. *My* piece of chocolate cake. The world seems to move into slow motion as the dinner lady scoops up the chocolatey wedge and hands it over to him.

"Noooooooooooooo..." I hear my own voice shrieking as if it is coming from somewhere far away.

Now, I'm not exactly proud of what happens next. I know in the grand scheme of things it is just a piece of cake, but *to be fair to me*, I am not having the best time; I've just had an argument with another horrible, rude boy, and that piece of cake was something I was really looking forward to, so the scene I am making is – at least a bit – outside of my own control. Also, if you think about it, that piece of cake was MINE, destined for me in a fair and square world if that horrible jerk hadn't pushed in front of me. You've got to stand up against these kinds of wrongs because before you know it people are stripping away your human rights left, right and centre. Yes, today it's a piece of chocolate cake but tomorrow it could be my right to a fair trial and then I could find myself rotting away in a prison cell, dreaming of chocolate cake while the rats gnaw on my weekly crust of bread and I maintain a dignified vow of silence and write searing letters that get printed in all the newspapers and start a revolution and then people camp outside the prison campaigning for my release.

Anyway, now is not the time for daydreaming, and my screech certainly seems to have made an impact. An uneasy hush falls over the canteen as curious eyes slide in our direction and the black blazer turns around to face me.

It belongs to a tall, and, I notice angrily, very good-looking boy. He has dark, silky hair, that sort of flops around his face like he's stumbled out of a boy band poster and smooth, acorn-coloured skin without a single spot on it. His dark eyes are widened in surprise, and I notice that he has a little mole at the side of his mouth like Marilyn Monroe. For a second I stand, stunned, my mouth hanging open as I stare into his perfect face. He is, I notice, surrounded by the baboon-ish football types. Fantastic.

"What's the matter with you?" he asks in alarm.

"You pushed in," I say, recovering my sense of dignity and righteous anger. My hand goes to my hip as I glare at him. "I was next in the queue but you pushed in. And now you've taken my piece of cake."

"*Your* cake?" the boy says, looking down at the slice of chocolatey goodness. A smirk seems to be tugging at his lips, and I'm starting to think maybe he's not so good-looking after all. "I think you'll find it's *my* cake." His voice is smug.

"Yes, but only because you pushed in," I say, mulishly. "It's not fair."

The boy seems to consider this for a moment, tipping his head to one side and elaborately tapping his cheek with his finger. "Hmm," he murmurs. "I see what you mean . . . except, of course. . ." He reaches into his blazer pocket and pulls out a little laminated card. The words LUNCH PASS glare back at me in red ink.

"What is that?" I ask.

The boy's smile grows and there's a giggle from one of the people behind him. In fact, there are quite a few people taking an interest in our conversation,

I notice. And quite a lot of them seem to be staring moonily at the boy in front of me.

"It's a lunch pass," he says slowly, as though explaining something to an idiot. "It means I can go to the front of the queue without waiting." He's really enjoying himself now.

I fold my arms across my chest. The queue behind me is getting restless, but I'm not moving. Not even when a voice from behind me yells, "Come on! Get out the way! Let us eat!"

"That's not fair," I say again, my attention focused on the boy. "Why do you have that?"

"You must be new," is the answer that I get.

"So what if I am?" I ask.

"Then you obviously don't know how this school works." The boy is starting to look bored now. "I'm the junior class president on the school council. I was elected last December. The lunch pass is one of the things you get when you're elected."

"A lunch pass?" I ask, my eyes narrowing "Why? So you can cut the queue? Why do you need one of those?"

The boy shrugs. "I don't know *why* you get one," he says. "You just do."

"But that's so stupid." I snort. "If you don't need it

then why do you get it?" And then the rest of what he said sinks in. "You?" I say, taking in his pretty face, the football boots hanging from his bag. This is a classic "cool kid". I know all the signs. I've seen it all this week. My eyes narrow. "*You're* the junior class president?"

The boy shrugs again. It seems to be very much his go-to gesture and he doesn't seem at all worried by my growing rage. "Yes," he says. "What's so funny about that?"

"Oh, nothing," I say sweetly. "I'd love to hear some of your policies."

The boy looks confused. "Policies?" he mutters. "What are you talking about?"

Exactly as I thought. This boy so obviously doesn't care about the student council; all he cares about are the perks that come with it – the kinds of perks that let you steal other people's cake. My indignation fans the flames of my anger even more. "Well, what do you actually DO then?" I ask.

There is a moment of silence and the boy looks at me. Then suddenly he smiles. "This," he says, and he grabs a fork off the side and digs it into the piece of chocolate cake.

My own eyes widen. I can't believe he's doing this. But he does. He loads up the fork with a huge chunk of cake and crams it into his mouth. "Mmm," he says, swallowing. "Delicious."

"I— I. . ." I splutter.

"That really is good cake," the boy says. "Shame you didn't get a piece." He licks his lips, catching a few stray crumbs. "I suppose you should have run for student council."

"WELL, MAYBE I WILL!" I hear a voice yell defiantly, and with a jolt I realize it is my own. I can't believe it's my voice. MY voice. A wave of hysterical laughter rises inside me and I push it down as fast as I can. Maybe this is actually a great idea, I think; maybe this is how I can make my big stand. How I can change things. How I can SET THE WORLD ALIGHT WITH MY ENTHUSIASM AND DEDICATION. As I grin up into this boy's face, I can feel my eyes going all wild like they did after that big cup of coffee.

My heart is thundering in my chest, and I draw myself up as tall as possible.

"Yes!" I say, and I wave my finger in his face. "Maybe that's exactly what I'll do. You said the elections were in December, right? Well, I'll run against you . . . and I'll win!"

The boy looks so flabbergasted that I laugh . . . the laugh comes out a bit high-pitched and manic sounding, but I'm really flying now, the adrenaline pumping through my veins. "SEE YOU ON THE CAMPAIGN TRAIL!" I cry, dropping my tray back on the side with a loud clatter and turning on my heel, walking briskly out of the now silent canteen on trembling legs.

CHAPTER *Four*

I steam through the corridor towards the girls' toilets. As I do so I can't help but notice that I'm passing a lot of people openly staring at me. It seems I had quite an audience inside the canteen . . . and outside it, if the volume of my rage was as high as I think it was. Pushing through the swinging door into the toilets, I surprise a group of girls clustered around the mirror, fluffing their hair and applying lip balm.

"What is the junior class president's name?" I gasp without thinking, my voice desperate and demanding. I sound like one of those people in time-traveller films who stumble around screeching, "WHAT YEAR IS THIS?"

The girls turn to stare at me, their mouths hanging open.

One of them is still frozen with her hairbrush embedded in her long, shiny hair. I catch a glimpse of myself in the mirror and my cheeks are red, my eyes a bit wild, my hair has reached critical levels of enormous. It's . . . not great.

I clear my throat and raise a trembling hand to try and smooth down some of my curls. "Sorry," I say in a more normal voice. "Um, I was just wondering if any of you know the name of the boy who is the junior class president on student council?"

The girls continue to stare, but the one with the dark hair retrieves her hairbrush and speaks to me in a slow, soothing voice, as though I am a skittish horse.

"His name is Aaron Davis," she says, and for a second I think the mere sound of his name is going to make them all swoon.

"Everyone knows that," one of her friends puts in here. She is looking at me like I am something nasty on the bottom of her shoe.

"Right," I say, turning to grasp the sink and looking at myself in the mirror. "Aaron Davis." I turn his name over in my mouth. It's not a great name for a nemesis, to be honest. It doesn't sound sinister enough. I'd rather he was called Evilborg Skeletrix or something like that. "Aaron Davis," I say again, making it sound as evil as possible. Over my shoulder I see the girl with dark hair mouthing the word "WOW" at her friends and they begin to edge carefully out of the room until I am left standing there alone. "I will defeat you, Aaron Davis." I make the vow to my own reflection, still imagining the terrible smirk on his face.

By the time I find myself walking home later that afternoon, the adrenaline has rubbed off and my stomach is rumbling loudly. It seems that I have gone from anonymous loner to notorious weirdo in the course of one lunch break. Wherever I go people whisper behind their hands and giggle. I'm not exactly sure what they're saying, but I think I get the gist. The scene I caused in the canteen has created quite a stir, and, whoever Aaron Davis is, he seems to have quite a following. I gnaw my lip nervously as I make my way along the street towards my house, trying to banish the image of his smug face from my thoughts.

"Something on your mind?" a voice calls as I

reach the front garden. It's Iris again, resplendent in a bobbly yellow jumper and a pair of green tasselled earrings.

"Bad day," I admit in a small voice.

Iris tips her head thoughtfully. "Any particular reason?" she asks.

"I might have accidentally decided to run for student council in a brand-new school where I don't know a single person, against a boy who seems to have his own personal fan club," I reply. When I say it all out loud like that it sounds pretty terrible. I can feel my chin wobbling as worry overwhelms me. Well, worry and hunger. My stomach makes a loud growling noise. "He ate my chocolate cake," I sniffle, sounding – even to my own ears – like a real baby.

Iris regards me coolly. "Well," she says after a moment, "you'd better come in for something to eat then."

"What?" I ask, surprised.

"Come and have a cup of tea with me if you want," Iris says. "Or don't. I don't really care either way." She shrugs carelessly, but the way she says it makes me think that she does care a little bit. Perhaps because I've been feeling so lonely myself I seem to be able to sniff it out in other people, like some sort of weird loneliness bloodhound, and my Spidey-senses are telling me that Iris would like some company.

"I'd better just tell my dad," I say, slowly. After all, what do I really know about the woman? She could be an axe murderer. I'm not sure that an axe murderer would wear yellow tasselly earrings and have bubblegum-pink hair, but that could be part of her axe-murdery plan to lull her victim into a false sense of security. And the fact that she's a little old lady is irrelevant; it would be sexist AND ageist to dismiss her axe-murderer potential based on that. I'm sure old ladies could be just as good at axe murdering as anyone else if they wanted to be. I eye her with suspicion.

"All right," Iris agrees in a very unconcerned and non-threatening voice. "You tell your dad and I'll leave the door on the latch for you."

I push open our front door and yell in to Dad that I'm popping next door for a cup of tea with our neighbour. He must be distracted by work because I just hear a vague noise of agreement and no further questions. Well, at least I've left a trail for the police, should it come to it.

When I make my way through Iris's front door, the house is not what I expected. I don't really know what I did expect exactly, but perhaps – given Iris's rather eccentric appearance, and the messy state of her front garden – I was anticipating something like a scene from that TV show where people are trapped in their homes by mountains of their own junk. Instead of being full of piles of junk, however, the house is cool and calm. A huge painting hangs in the light, airy hallway. It is a messy riot of different colours, and when I look at it, it makes me feel more cheerful.

"Hellooooo," I call, tiptoeing further into the hallway.

"In here," Iris's voice drifts through, and I follow the sound into the kitchen, at the back of the house. The walls in here are painted a bright, hot pink and at first it takes my breath away a bit, and then I realize it's actually warm and cosy and the feeling of happiness increases. It looks less and less likely that Iris is an axe-wielding murderer.

"Sit down." Iris gestures to a seat at a long kitchen table. She is tottering around the kitchen now, gathering tea things together and (I am very pleased to see) pulling a large packet of custard creams out of her cupboard. Her movements are slow and trembly, and she is even smaller than I first thought, her body slightly stooped.

"WANT A SCRATCH?" a loud, gravelly voice shouts, causing me to jump about two metres out of my seat.

Maybe the murdering ideas aren't so far-fetched after all.

"Be quiet, Lennon!" Iris snaps. "We've got a guest."

I turn slowly to look behind me and see a large birdcage where a grey parrot is perched on a stand, eyeing me suspiciously.

"STUPID MOON HEAD!" the bird croaks.

"I don't think he likes me," I say nervously, and glumness seeps through my whole body. Even birds are being very open about how much they hate me now. What chance do I have with humans?

Iris cackles, handing me my mug of tea. "Don't take it personally. He's a very rude bird. That's why we get on so well." Iris hobbles over and hands Lennon a nut, which he takes very gently with what I can't help but notice are rather sharp-looking talons. Lennon dips his head politely and gives a loud wolf whistle before tucking into his treat.

"Now," Iris says, dropping into the seat across from me with an audible sigh of relief, "what was all that about running for student council?"

"Oh, it's nothing really," I say, and then, when Iris remains quiet, I fill her in on the scene in the canteen. To be honest it's quite nice to have someone to talk to about it.

"Sounds like that boy needed taking down a peg," Iris says finally.

"HOPELESS LOSER!" Lennon chimes in.

"Well, yes," I agree, "but it was still a silly thing to do. I don't even know how the whole thing works. How can I hope to win over the entire school when I can't even seem to make one single friend?"

Iris fixes me with a beady stare. "That sounds like an awful lot of feeling sorry for yourself to me."

"Well, I suppose I *am* feeling pretty sorry for myself," I admit. "I'm normally a very positive person, but moving school has been a lot harder than I thought it would be. I don't know what I was thinking... I guess I'll have to back out, and hope everyone forgets all about it." I can feel tears gathering behind my eyes and I stare down at the table, trying to push them back.

"It sounds to me like throwing yourself into a big project could be just what you need," Iris says then. "After all, there must be an election, and some rules for you to follow. You seem a clever enough girl." She makes a sort of snorting sound here as though she's not completely sure about this but has decided to give me the benefit of the doubt. "I'm sure you could work it out. Then you just take it one step at a time."

I sit up a bit at that, nodding slowly. I *do* like a big project. Just think of the highlighters. . . I've had my eye on some new ones in pastel shades. The first little twinkling of excitement fizzes inside me. I think Iris must see it because she gives me a small smile. "Sounds like this school could use a girl with a bit of vision," she says. "Is that you, though?"

"Oh, I've got vision," I reply firmly. "Sometimes I feel like I've got too much of it." The tingling feeling is growing inside me. After all, it's not hopeless, is it? I've got six weeks to win over my fellow students, and that's loads of time. Just think about all the good things I could achieve. Like doing away with lunch passes for the privileged few, and setting up more clubs and activities so that people don't have to eat their lunch alone. And that's just the tip of the iceberg. This could be the first step on my path to prime minister. One day I'll be chatting with Hillary Rodham Clinton (who will be remarkably well-preserved for her age) and I'll say to her, "Of course, Hillary, it all began with a little school election. Who'd have thought then that I would become the youngest British prime minister in history?" and Hillary will laugh and pour me another cup of coffee (which I will be very used to by then) and offer to write the introduction to my new book about leadership.

"Where have you gone?" Iris's voice breaks into my daydream. "You're looking all glazed over."

"Just thinking about being prime minister," I say.

"Well, you'd better win *this* election first," Iris sniffs. "Still, we could do with a decent prime minister. I'd vote for you."

"Would you?" I ask, and I can feel a huge grin spreading across my face.

"I would," Iris says shortly. "So you'd better get on with it."

CHAPTER *Five*

By the time I leave Iris's house it's getting dark outside and my head is buzzing. I am feeling so inspired by my chat with Iris that I'm beginning to think this race for student council president wasn't such a bad idea. In fact, perhaps it's my DESTINY. Yes, the more I think about it, the more I am convinced that it's my calling, my *duty* to come to the aid of Highworth Grange secondary school. To give them a president worthy of their vote, one who really cares, one who will champion the underdog, one who will stride down the corridors (which will NOT be full of people's bags) discussing important plans with her trusted advisors. (Note to self: probably make some friends first who can be trusted advisors. Sigh.)

I find Lil slumped on the floor in front of the telly.

"How's it going?" I ask.

"Can I get A BIT of peace and quiet, please," Lil responds grumpily. "You know I like silence when my programmes are on."

"Lovely," I say, flopping on to the sofa.

"There you are," Dad says as he comes into the room. Lil shoots him an evil look that he ignores. "Did you say you were at the neighbour's house?"

"Yep." I yawn and stretch my arms above my head. "Iris invited me in for tea. She's really cool," I add.

"Iris." Dad's forehead crumples. "Oh, the lady with the pink hair. Yes, she seems . . . interesting."

"I told her she could borrow my *Frozen* DVD," Lil says without turning away from the screen. "Can you believe she's actually never seen it? It's like she is from another planet or something."

"How was school?" Dad says, changing the subject.

I shrug. "The usual," I say lightly. I decide not to tell him about my stand-off with Aaron or my run for office. After all, it's not a done deal and I haven't even found out the rules yet.

Dad puts a hand on my shoulder and gives it a squeeze. "Just keep swimming, *Effitsa*," he says quietly.

We are interrupted then by the commotion that accompanies Mum's arrival home. There's a lot of slamming and banging as she staggers in with pink cheeks and three tote bags full of heavy books and a backpack spilling papers everywhere. I eye the loose papers with a shudder – I obviously did not get my supreme organizational skills from my mum.

"Coffee!" she gasps as she collapses on to the sofa beside me, and Dad disappears to make her a big mug.

"Bad day?" I ask.

Mum groans. "Spent the whole afternoon wrestling with noun declensions and getting nowhere." She looks glum. Sometimes the poet she's working on seems determined to stump her by writing in Latin and Mum gets all stressed out and her dark curly hair gets bigger and curlier the more wound up she becomes. That is actually something we have in common; that and our light bronze skin, hazel eyes and love of orange Smarties. Today we both have hair so big I'm surprised we can fit side by side on the sofa.

Dad hands Mum her steaming mug and squeezes her hand. "Dinner will be ready in ten minutes," he says. "Shall we sit at the table or have it on our laps?"

"On our laps," we all chorus. Lil punches the air

happily. Slumpy dinner in front of the TV is a rare treat in our house.

Later on when we are all tucking into our lemony chicken, Mum looks up as if she's seeing me for the first time.

"Oh, Effie!" she exclaims. "I almost forgot. I've got an invitation for you."

"An invitation?" I ask, squeezing some extra lemon juice on to my food. "An invitation to what?"

"Here." Mum reaches into the pocket of her slightly bobbly cardigan and pulls out an envelope before handing it to me.

Inside the envelope is a piece of thin card. It really is an invitation.

DEAR:

_____

You are invited to a fancy-dress party to celebrate Katie's thirteenth birthday! —

See you there!

Venue: 27 Green Lane   Date: Sat 22 Oct   Time: 5-8.30

I turn the invitation over in my hands. "What is this?" I ask Mum.

"Turns out that one of my new colleagues from work has a daughter in your school and she's having a birthday party on Saturday. They'd love you to go and I thought it might be a good way for you to meet some people." Mum is looking really pleased with herself.

"Are you sure?" I ask doubtfully. "The invitation doesn't even have my name on. It's just blank."

"Oh, Katie must have forgotten to fill it out." Mum shrugs. "It'll be fun." She smiles at me hopefully. "We can sort out a really good costume for you."

"I guess," I say. I have to admit that the invitation makes me feel nervous. I don't even know who this Katie is. There are a couple of Katies in my classes, but it might not even be one of them at all. Going to a party where you don't know anyone is not exactly the most exciting prospect.

Dad must be reading my mind because he pipes up in a cheery voice. "It can be really difficult to meet new people at school," he says. "You're always in lessons and running around from place to place. This way you'll get to really talk to people and it will be much more relaxed."

"Maybe." I frown.

"And if you hate it, I'll come right back and get you," Dad promises.

"Really?" I ask.

"We both will," Mum says, squeezing my arm. "But you'll see, it will be great." She sounds so absolutely certain that some of her certainty starts to rub off on me.

"You're right." I pull my shoulders back and lift my chin. "It'll be the perfect opportunity to make some new friends." And, I add silently, the perfect place to kick-start my campaign for student council president. After all, loads of networking happens at parties, doesn't it? I can see myself now, standing in the middle of a little crowd, all of my new friends hanging on my every word.

"Who's that?" someone will whisper.

"That's Effie Kostas," the reply will come. "She's going to be our new student council president."

A spontaneous burst of applause will follow, and I will nod and smile modestly.

"What about a costume?" Dad asks, interrupting my thoughts. "Any ideas what you want to go as?"

"Oh yes," I grin. "I've got a brilliant idea."

CHAPTER *Six*

When I arrive at the party the next evening I ring the doorbell and it is opened by a girl I recognize. It's the Katie from my English class, so I deduce she must be the birthday girl.

"Hi!" I say brightly, thrusting the neatly wrapped gift in my hands (a new pencil case and some fancy scented biros) at her. "Happy birthday!"

Katie looks a little stunned. "Hi," she says.

It is at this point that I can't help but notice she is wearing a denim miniskirt, a strappy red top and a pair of sparkly red devil horns. It is not exactly a huge effort as costumes go.

I clamp one hand on my wide-brimmed hat to keep it from blowing off. I don't really know what to say next as I am still standing on the doorstep. I clear my throat anxiously.

"Well, I guess you'd better come in then," my gracious hostess mutters.

As I wrestle with my skirts, trying to get into the house, I get the first inkling that I might have overdone it on the costume front.

"Who are you?" Katie asks, running an eye over my outfit.

I pull my VOTES FOR WOMEN sign from where it is tucked under my arm and show it off. "I'm Millicent Garrett Fawcett," I say, and her eyes widen a little. "You know, the suffragist?" I add when Katie continues to look confused.

"Right." Katie's voice sounds a bit strangled. "I actually meant who are YOU?"

"Oh." I try not to feel too crushed; after all, it's probably hard to recognize me in my rather brilliant costume. "I'm Effie. I'm new to Highworth Grange, but I'm in your English class." I beam at her. There's quite a long pause. "Our mums work together?" The last bit sounds like a question because Katie is still looking a little mystified and I'm starting to wonder if I've accidentally come to the wrong house. After all, there are lots of people called Katie, and the devil horns could just be a fashion statement that I don't yet know about.

Before I can worry too much about this, though, Katie's face clears. "Oh yeah." She shrugs. "The new girl." Her eyes gleam and she looks more closely at me. "You're the one who got into that big scene with Aaron in the canteen."

Aaron. Evil Aaron. "Well," I say carefully, "I wouldn't exactly call it a scene. . ." I know that it's bad form to slam your political rivals so I try to be polite, and instead of pointing out that that Aaron boy was a big rude bully, I say, "It was more of an . . . um . . . spirited exchange of views."

Katie's eyes narrow as she takes this in. "Well, you should come through," she says finally, gesturing through to the living room.

Here I find a handful of other students who I vaguely recognize gathered together in small groups. There is music playing quite loudly, something without any lyrics, just a pulsing bass line. Along one wall is a long table covered in plates piled high with sandwiches and sausage rolls, and bottles of Coke and lemonade. Katie instantly disappears again, back to answer the doorbell.

I paste on a smile and smooth my skirt, trying to

pluck up the courage to introduce myself to someone. Apart from one boy who is wearing a sort-of makeshift pirate outfit, no one seems to have made much effort on the costume front. I'm not going to give in straight away, but the desire to phone Dad to ask him to turn around and get me is strong. I pull back my shoulders. *Come on, Effie*, I say to myself. *You can do this. You can make a friend. One little friend, that's all you need. You're going to have to toughen up if you want to be a real leader.* I can't help feeling a pang of loneliness, though.

The loneliness only increases as the room begins to fill up around me and I hover uncertainly by the food, picking pieces of pineapple off skewers so that I can just eat the lumps of cheese.

"Hello!" I exclaim as the boy in the pirate costume bears down on the sausage rolls. "This cheese is nice!"

The boy shies away from me as though I am some kind of dangerous criminal.

"It's cheddar, I think!" I beam encouragingly. "Although I'm partial to a bit of Edam myself."

"What are you on about?" he says gruffly, staring at me from under a pair of quite bushy eyebrows.

"CHEEEEESE," I say loudly and slowly, as he

seems to be having difficulty grasping the basic fundamentals of making conversation.

The boy boggles again, his eyes sweeping over me to take in the lacy yards of material that make up my costume. "Weirdo," he mutters finally, darting past me to grab a sausage roll in his meaty fist and then turning away.

I sigh. Not a promising start.

I try to make conversation with a couple more people when they come to get their drinks, but they seem a bit startled by my costume. Perhaps I should take off the hat? It is quite wide. We made it out of the one Mum sometimes wears to weddings and it's a bit big for me.

Just as I'm about to give up, a voice pipes up from beside me. "I like your costume."

I swing around to find myself facing a small girl with a goatee. Further examination reveals that the goatee has been drawn on with eyeliner. Her fair hair is pulled back in a low ponytail. She is wearing a pair of pale trousers tucked into riding boots, a waistcoat with a white lacy ruffle poking out the top and a long blue coat with shining gold buttons.

"Oh wow!" I exclaim. "You're Alexander Hamilton!" *Hamilton* is my favourite musical. It's sort of about this orphan who climbs his way to the top and helps America to beat Britain in the American revolution but it's mostly about these really cool sisters who are all clever and noisy and think women should have the same rights as men. It's brilliant and the music . . . is . . . the . . . BEST.

The girl grins at me and her grin is a friendly, shining beacon of joy.

I can feel a glow spreading through me, right into

the tops of my ears and my fingertips. Is it possible that I have finally found a potential friend?

"I'm Effie," I say.

"Angelika," the girl replies. "I actually thought about coming as Angelica from *Hamilton*, but I worried the big skirts might get in the way."

"You're not wrong there," I mutter, tugging at my dress again.

Angelika laughs. "Plus I thought I'd rock the goatee."

"Well, you were right about that too," I say. "It's a really good costume."

"So is yours." Angelika's face is approving.

"I'm glad someone likes it," I say quickly. "I don't know anyone and you're the first person to talk to me all afternoon."

"Don't worry," Angelika grins, showing off very straight, pearly white teeth. "I won't abandon you. I'm so glad there's someone to talk to – I thought this party was going to be SO boring."

"Why did you come then?" I ask, puzzled.

Angelika rolls her eyes. "My parents made me. My dad works with Katie's dad. We've known each other since we were little, we used to be really good friends actually." She frowns here, her eyes flickering in Katie's direction. "Not so much after we started secondary school though."

"Do you go to Highworth Grange?" I ask hopefully. Maybe this really is the pal I've been looking for. "I don't remember seeing you around."

"I've been off for the last couple of weeks," Angelika says. "Some gross flu-type thing that had snot exploding out of my face. I'm better now!" she exclaims, catching the flicker of alarm in my eyes. "So, you must be new then?"

"Yes," I say with a heavy sigh. "It's been pretty rubbish actually, not knowing anyone."

"Well, you know me now." Angelika smiles, and it's like the sun peeking out from behind the clouds. I've made a friend! My first new friend. I'm suddenly very glad that I let Mum and Dad talk me into coming.

Angelika and I chat for a while, not about anything particularly important. It is easy and relaxed, and at one point she has me laughing so hard that tears stream down my face and I clutch my stomach, unable to breathe. It's the kind of laugh that really seals a friendship, like the perfect cherry on an ice cream sundae.

I tell Angelika about how I've been moping around the school alone, about how horrible eating lunch by myself has been. "I think there should be more ways to stop people from feeling lonely at school," I say. "Like having a mentor to show you around and introduce you to people and make sure you don't have to sit by yourself and feel like an outcast." Angelika is nodding in agreement. "And," I add, warming to the subject, "there should be way more clubs and activities happening at lunch breaks. . . That way people would have more places to go and meet new people outside of lessons."

"Yeah, you're definitely right about that." Angelika nods again and slurps some lemonade from her glass. "I'm the secretary on the student council," she says, and I perk up at this. Finally, someone on the inside. Now I might be able to find out a bit more about how things work. "We're supposed to be in charge of the funding for the clubs and societies," Angelika continues, "but the money always ends up going to the boys' sports teams." She sighs, and I can hear my heart thumping in my ears.

"The boys' sports teams?" I repeat dangerously.

"Oh yeah," Angelika says. "*They're* always OK, because the captain of the football team and all his pals run the council. I vote against them a lot, but it doesn't make much difference."

"I can't believe it!" I yelp. "Aaron Davis is more evil than I originally thought! Our school is being run by a corrupt government!" I shake my head. "Now I really need to win," I say, almost to myself.

"Wait!" Angelika exclaims. "You're the girl who had the big fight with Aaron Davis in the canteen over a piece of cake?" She smacks her head with her hand. "Of course you are!"

I groan. "It wasn't really a big fight," I say. "And how did you even hear about it if you haven't been at school?"

"No, no, I think it's brilliant!" Angelika interrupts. "Everyone was talking about it when I arrived. He's so arrogant, no one in the school ever stands up to him."

"He did seem like a bit of a jerk," I say, forgetting my resolution to keep things civil.

"Oh, he is," Angelika agrees. "He and Katie make a perfect pair. I'm surprised he's not here actually." She swings around, eyeing up the crowd that has built up around us.

"He knows Katie?" I ask.

"Yeah." Angelika nods. "They're sort of girlfriend and boyfriend ... well, sometimes. He's the year above us, of course, so he's got a huuuuuge fan club in our year."

"Oh." I let that sink in. "I'm a bit worried," I admit, after a moment. "Because I did sort of threaten to run against him for junior student president."

"What, really? That's what the fight was really about?" Angelika's eyes gleam.

"Yes," I say, "but I didn't exactly think it through. I'm not completely sure where to start. It's pretty tough to run a whole campaign by yourself when you don't know anyone . . . and no one knows you."

"Well, you don't have to worry about doing it alone any more, do you?" Angelika quirks an eyebrow and throws her arms wide open. "You've got a campaign manager . . . me!"

CHAPTER *Seven*

I think Mum and Dad are almost as relieved as me when I tell them about meeting Angelika on the way home. Even Lil, who is strapped into the back seat of the car, gives a cheer and starts chanting, "EFFIE HAS A FRIEND, EFFIE HAS A FRIEND, EFFIE ISN'T GOING TO DIE ALOOOOOOONE," which is, I guess, a nice sentiment, if a little extreme.

I settle back and lean my forehead against the cool window, my oversized hat flung on to the seat between us, replaying the afternoon in my head. It wasn't just Angelika's enthusiasm for the campaign that made me feel better. Sometimes you meet someone and you know straight away that the two of you are going to be friends. It's as if your brains are sending out matching wiggly brainwaves and your ideas fall all over each other and you can't talk fast enough because you want to say EVERYTHING to each other all at once.

Angelika and I are going to start laying out our plans on Monday and I am already fizzing over with ideas. Talking about the campaign has left me feeling so inspired. I may have been dragged into this by a fight over a piece of cake, but now that I'm here I'm starting to see all the different ways that I could make a difference, the ways me and Angelika could work as a team to make our school a better place. All we have to do is find out all the rules and all the different steps to create a smooth path to victory. I asked Angelika at the party why she wasn't running for president herself, but she said she's more of a behind-the-scenes kind of person.

"What we need," she said with a grin, "is someone who isn't afraid to make a bit of noise." She tipped her head to one side. "Are you ready to be extra noisy, Effie Kostas?"

"I WAS BORN READY!" I yelled, and heads turned in our direction as the two of us burst into giggles again.

It's just so exciting, and funny how sharing the idea of the campaign with someone else has made it seem so much more manageable. Now, I realize, I'm actually looking forward to going back to school.

The weekend passes in a blur of unpacking. It looks like we're finally finished, and with all the boxes out of the way, our little wonky house, truly feels like home. Dad makes banana pancakes with maple syrup on Sunday morning to celebrate, and even yet another mandatory viewing of *Frozen* is not enough to dampen my good mood. In fact, as I snuggle under a blanket on the sofa, watching Lil's lips move in time with every single word, I feel a warm sense of happiness and purpose that I haven't felt for a while. I feel like me again. Not sad, lonely Effie, but really, properly me. I'm back, baby!

The Highworth Grange Chronicle

Issue No. 201

MYSTERY GIRL IN CONFRONTATION WITH STUDENT PRESIDENT

By Catriona McGiddens

... Students were left **STUNNED** on Thursday when an unknown girl got into a very **LOUD** and **AGGRESSIVE** argument with junior student council president, Aaron Davis. I spoke to several witnesses who described the girl as "quite small" but with "properly enormous hair". It would seem that the argument erupted over a piece of cake, although reports differ as to what *kind* of cake was at the centre of the brawl. "It was carrot cake," one source insisted, while another claimed they would "bet my chicken nuggets it was **VICTORIA SPONGE**". Whatever the cause of the showdown, everyone agreed that it concluded with the unknown girl threatening to run against Aaron for president. Who is this mystery girl? Will she really run? And does she have a dangerous obsession with baked goods? **ONLY TIME WILL TELL...**

My Monday gets off to a great start when I arrive to find Angelika waiting for me at the school gates. "Hi!" she calls.

"Hi!" I reply with a grin. "I almost didn't recognize you without the goatee."

Angelika strokes her chin sadly. "I actually quite liked it," she confesses.

"Me too," I agree, and we make our way into the main building.

It turns out that Angelika is in almost all of my

classes, and when she carefully unpacks not one, not two, but *three* different coloured binders bristling with neon Post-it notes I almost get to my feet and applaud.

When lunchtime rolls around Angelika and I head to the library to try to find out the rules for running for election. The library has been one of the safe places that I've been escaping to during my lonely first weeks. It is warm and cosy and full of books – perfect if you're feeling sad and on your own.

Since we don't have a proper librarian any more (a complete CRIME, if you ask me, and something that I would definitely take a good look at if I were prime minister) the teachers take it in turns to man the desk on their lunch break. Today Miss Sardana is in there, wearily slurping at a bowl of soup. She seems a bit surprised by our question about the election.

"Hmm," she says thoughtfully. "I'm not exactly sure what the rules are." Her eyes narrow. "We haven't had a proper election before, I don't think. Honestly, girls, I think most years there's only one person who runs. Sometimes no one runs at all and then the teachers have to try and persuade someone to volunteer. Are you sure it's something you really want to do? As I understand it, Aaron is happy to run again, so there's no need."

"Well, I think there's a need!" I exclaim hotly. "This year there's a high-stakes bitter rivalry at the centre of things, and an evil tyrant to defeat, so we definitely need to know all the rules."

"In that case I expect you need the school handbook," Miss Sardana sighs, apparently not moved by my urgent tone.

"Of course!" Angelika smacks her hand against her forehead. "How could I not have thought of that? Do you have one here?"

"I think so." Miss Sardana reluctantly pushes her soup to one side. "Hang on, and I'll go and get it from the office."

When she returns, Angelika and I take the folder from her and sit at a table before diving in. Whoever wrote the school handbook did a pretty terrible job. There's no logical flow and no handy index, not even some well-placed multicoloured dividers. I tsk over this, pointing it out to Angelika, who groans in agreement. Finally, we track down the page we have been looking for and I copy the relevant rules neatly into my notebook. They look like this:

- All candidates who wish to run for student council must add their names to the sign-up sheet by the specified date.
- Candidates for junior and senior president will take part in a debate outlining their vision for the role.
- Candidates for junior and senior president may campaign using posters and/or flyers in approved areas.
- Candidates for junior and senior president are required to hold a stall at the student fair to raise money for the PTA. This is a demonstration of both the community spirit and organizational skills that are fundamental to the position.
- The election will take place during morning registration on an agreed-upon date before the Christmas break. Students in years 7-9 will vote for junior council positions, years 10-11 for senior council positions. The votes will be counted by group tutors and tallied and announced in an assembly later that afternoon.

It isn't exactly like running for prime minister, but

at least now I can see that there are different steps that we can work towards. Some of the points are a bit vague. . . I don't know what the student fair is, and there are no actual dates on this, so I guess we'll have to ask someone else about that. I glance over at Miss Sardana, but I think we've taken up enough of her lunch break for today. There's one other point further down the page that I notice and make a note of.

- Student councils will be responsible for the distribution of petty cash to all extra-curricular clubs and societies.

Well, Angelika was right, that certainly explains why the football team are raking in the funds. I blow out a slow, angry breath. NOT ON MY WATCH, AARON DAVIS, my internal voice shouts, and I feel my fist clenching as though it's about to wave dramatically at the skies. The more I find out about the job of junior class president, the more I see that it is wasted on evil Aaron. Just think about all the good he could be doing, all the responsibilities he is just ignoring. Someone needs to take a stand, and that someone is definitely going to be me.

We gather our stuff and head to the canteen with

some speed to make sure we don't miss out on getting something to eat for lunch. Angelika introduces me to a few of her friends. They're not in the same classes as us so I haven't seen them around, but Angelika has been pals with most of them since primary school. At first I feel a bit nervous about meeting them. I've only got one friend, after all, and I can't really afford to share her. But the others seem really nice too, and we spend most of the lunch break chatting. There's one girl in particular called Jess who I get on well with. Jess is tall, with long red hair that falls in thick waves down her back. Her pale face is covered in freckles and her eyes are a greyish green colour. She talks in quite a loud, flat voice and doesn't seem to like making eye contact with people. That doesn't get in the way of us bonding over our shared love of musicals and videos of dogs being reunited with their owners.

As we sit talking away I can feel myself starting to relax. Looking around the canteen I finally stop seeing it as some kind of horrible wasteland where I find myself alone and miserable, and instead I take a moment to enjoy the cheerful chatter, the warm glow of the fluorescent lights, the weirdly comforting smell of school dinners. My moment of calm is broken when a familiar figure walks past. It is Aaron Davis – he of the perfectly floppy hair and air of extreme entitlement. His eyes don't even twitch in my direction, but I notice that Katie is beside him, clamping his fingers firmly between her own, and she *does* treat me to a smirk and a toss of her glossy brown hair.

Angelika snorts. "Looks like those two are back together again." A mischievous gleam enters her eyes. "HI, KATIE!" she shouts without even a pinch of warning to me. "I NEED TO TALK TO YOU!"

Grudgingly, Katie swings around and Aaron, still superglued to her side by the apparently unbreakable hand-holding, is forced to join her.

"What is it?" Katie huffs.

"Not a big deal," Angelika sings sweetly. "I just wondered if I left my duelling pistol at your house?"

Katie looks startled, and so does Aaron. In fact, he's eyeing my new friend with something that looks a bit like fear. *Good*, I think, hiding a smile behind my hand. "What?" Katie manages.

"It's not a real one, obviously," Angelika explains patiently. "I made it, as part of my costume."

"Oh." Katie's face clears. "No, I haven't seen it." She shrugs. "Must have been chucked away with the decorations."

"Oh, and you remember Effie, don't you?" Angelika gestures to me, and I choke a little on my chocolate milk.

"Yeah." Katie barely glances at me. "Hi."

"Hello!" I exclaim, trying to look friendly.

"We didn't see you at the party, Aaron," Angelika says, and I dare to look over at him. Our eyes meet, and for a second I feel the crackle of dislike zapping between us like an angry electric shock.

"I couldn't make it," he mutters. "Homework."

"Which you didn't even need to do," Katie says then, and she sounds a bit grumpy, as if they've already been fighting about it. "You know the teachers always give you extra time because of football practice."

"They do WHAT?" I explode, and Katie and Aaron eye me nervously. "Let me guess," I snap, "the girls' netball team don't get the same treatment."

"The girls' netball team aren't the defending league

champions." Katie tosses her hair again, as if that puts an end to any argument.

"Unbelievable," I mutter.

Aaron just continues to look bored.

Angelika turns to Jess. "Did Effie tell you that she's running against Aaron for junior class president this year?" she asks casually.

"No, she didn't tell me," Jess says in her loud voice. "But she'll never beat Aaron." Aaron's face fills with a look of annoying self-satisfaction at this. "He's not very clever," Jess continues, as if Aaron isn't standing right in front of her, "but people seem to vote for him anyway." Aaron's smirk slips a bit.

"Well, you never know." Angelika smiles serenely. "This year could be different."

"That's true," I say, plucking up my courage and drawing back my shoulders. "After all. . ." I turn to him. "You've never run against me before."

"Can we go now?" Aaron says to Katie in a put-upon voice, ignoring me completely and tugging at her hand.

"Of course," Katie says.

"Guess some people can't handle a little friendly competition," I smile.

Aaron's eyes slide over in my direction. "There's no

competition about it," he says in a bored voice. "I'm going to wipe the floor with you. I don't know why you're even bothering."

He sounds completely sure of himself, as if there's nothing anyone could do to take the victory from him. As if it's all already his and he doesn't even have to try. I feel my fingers curl into my palms, but I force myself to smile. "I guess I'm bothering because I think it matters," I say lightly. "I think the best candidate should win. Maybe that's you . . . but maybe it's not."

"We'll see," is all Aaron says, but his mouth is set in a thin line.

"Yes," I say, and my voice is strong, certain – I feel like this is a momentous statement, as if an enormous orchestra should be playing dramatic, stirring music behind me as I get slowly to my feet. "I suppose we will."

CHAPTER *Eight*

A week later, things finally get real. We have a big assembly in the enormous school hall and our head teacher, Ms Shaarawi, stands at the front and calls all the current junior student council members to the stage. When Aaron steps up, the polite applause suddenly gets loud and rowdy. There are noisy whoops from a huddle of boys at the back who spring to their feet, and Aaron grins at them, clasping his hands together and shaking them in the air, like he's a big champ, which makes me want to growl like an angry dog.

"Yes, thank you," Ms Shaarawi says. "Settle down, please." The boys at the back sit down and the student council members hover to one side.

"So," Ms Shaarawi continues, "as you know, we will be electing a new student council in just a few weeks' time. The student council is an important part of our school, and running for a spot is a good way to make a difference for your fellow students. It will also reflect well on your school record, and give you an insight into how important hard work and being part of a team can be." She looks over her glasses at the rows of students in front of her. "If you are interested in running for any of the positions, please sign up on the sheets pinned to the noticeboards in reception." She turns to the group currently standing onstage and smiles at them. "And I would like to thank our current student council for all their hard work over the last year. They did a great job, throwing a junior prom that I think will not easily be forgotten." There are whoops and cheers again here and a long round of applause before the assembly wraps up.

Junior prom? Parties are good things, don't get me wrong, but surely a student council could have more to show for itself by the end of the year? I squirm in my seat, imagining all that could be achieved, imagining the difference I could make. For starters, how about distributing the money more evenly so that everyone gets a chance to join a club or society that they're interested in?

As I file out of the assembly with everyone else, my head is spinning with ideas. *I have to win first*, I remind myself, and I must admit that running against Aaron is a little intimidating, even for me. In the last week I have only become more aware of how popular he is. He's in year nine now, but he was elected as president when he was in year eight like I am, and he was the first year-eight student president we ever had. He's the captain of the football team, and he *literally* has a fan club of girls in year seven who follow him around in their lunch breaks and pick bits of his rubbish out of the bin. I mean, I suppose we all need a hobby, but that seems a bit odd to me.

As for me and Aaron, we haven't spoken again since the lunchtime run-in with him and Katie. Every so often we'll catch each other's eye and I swear I hear the sound effects for two swords smashing together. Unfortunately, keeping him at a distance doesn't seem to be an option when I actually run into him in the corridor after assembly. I am walking with Angelika and chatting away when I feel a shoulder bash into mine.

"Ooof!" I exclaim as we ricochet off each other like we're inside a pinball machine.

"Oh, sorry, I didn't—" I start to say until I realize who it is.

"Kostas." Aaron's voice is icy.

"Davis," I spit, jerking my head in a little nod.

"Apology accepted." He stretches his mouth out into a smile that shows off white, shiny teeth, but which doesn't reach his eyes.

"It was just an automatic response," I snap, my hands on my hips. "It's called being polite. I once apologized to a chair that I bumped into."

Aaron snorts at this and I shoot him my best withering stare. "I notice you didn't apologize for bashing into me," I huff.

"Why would I?' Aaron shrugs and starts to walk away. "You're the one who wasn't looking where you were going."

I stand still, glaring at his back as he saunters off. Fury is bubbling inside me like a potent witch's brew in a steamy cauldron. He's so full of himself. I want to beat him so badly.

The only person who wants it as much is Angelika, who is spluttering indignantly beside me. Over the past week we've been hanging out non-stop. Like me, Angelika has big plans for her future. She wants to be a world-class surgeon, and she's already thinking about getting into university. She thinks running my campaign will beef out her application, and she's going to run for secretary again so that we can combine our votes to get some changes made around here. We have so much in common that we've quickly become inseparable, but it's not just that . . . it's that she really *believes* in making a difference. When I go on long rants about the importance of democracy, about how we can do anything we set our minds to, and how – even though we are young – we can change things for the better, Angelika doesn't roll her eyes at me like some people do. She gets to her feet and cheers. She makes me feel ten feet tall. I guess that's the sign of a good friend.

So it's no surprise that she accompanies me during morning break to sign up for junior class president. In fact, she pulls out her mobile phone – even though we're not supposed to have them on during school hours – and plays "The Story of Tonight" from *Hamilton* at the loudest possible volume on its tinny speaker as I solemnly scrawl my name on the sheet. It feels momentous. I dot the "I" in Effie with a star.

Angelika takes a picture of the sheet so that one day we can put it in my biography.

I am the first person to put my name on the list, but I know that won't be the case for long. I wonder if anyone else will run apart from Aaron? As I feel the familiar stirrings of panic in my chest I take a deep breath and try to think about what Iris said. Just taking things one step at a time. The next logical step, of course, is that we need somewhere to hold our first official campaign meeting. Now that we know the rules of campaigning we need to get started on strategizing properly. I raise the issue with Angelika.

"I suppose we could ask a teacher if we could use their classroom during lunchtimes and things?" Angelika crinkles her nose.

"Hmm," I murmur, not really convinced. "It would be better if we had a real space . . . a proper campaign office that we could call our own."

"Yeah," Angelika agrees, immediately grasping my vision. "The room where it happens."

"Exactly," I say. I mull this over for a second. "Maybe we should ask Miss Sardana if she has any ideas."

"Good plan." Angelika nods. "Let's go and find her."

CHAPTER *Nine*

"A campaign office?" Miss Sardana's brow creases. She still looks very worn out and I'm beginning to think the frown is a permanent facial feature.

"Yes." I nod eagerly. "Somewhere to strategize, hold meetings, work on the issues ... you know, normal campaign stuff."

"Well, Effie, we don't usually give students offices to run their campaign for junior class president... It's not exactly..." Miss Sardana trails off here, and I employ my special, wide-eyed pleading face. It's been working pretty well for me, ever since the successful dance mat gift acquisition of my fifth birthday. Mum and Dad never stood a chance.

"But, miss," Angelika chips in here, "that's because

people haven't taken it properly seriously before. That's one of the things Effie wants to change."

"Exactly," I agree, making a mental note that should she change her mind about being a surgeon, Angelika will make a very valuable head of communications when I am prime minister.

"I just don't know where we would find the space, girls." Miss Sardana shrugs wearily, spreading her fingers in a gesture to convey that the situation is out of her hands.

"There must be somewhere," I press, because if I am about to fall at the very first hurdle, then I truly don't deserve to call myself junior class president of Highworth Grange Secondary School. "Just somewhere really small. It doesn't have to be fancy, just private . . . a space we can use." I'm speaking softly now, trying to hypnotize her with my words. My eyes are getting wider and wider and I imagine the pupils spinning around in a rather mesmerizing fashion. To be honest, all this pleading is starting to make my head hurt, and I blink rapidly.

Miss Sardana gives me a slightly puzzled look and then seems to realize that the fastest way to get rid of us is to help us get what we need. "Does it have to have windows?" she asks finally, her voice reluctantly squeezed out of her.

"Windows?" I jump on her words, sensing weakness. "No! Windows, yuck! Who needs them? All that sunlight with its blinding rays. So distracting. We need something that's more private and secret, like a bunker."

Actually, I can see it all now . . . the secret service officers standing, silent but deeply respectful, outside the door as I use my palm print and retina scan to gain access to the dimly lit room. There, world leaders wait on-screen to congratulate me on my plan for world peace. "It was no more than my duty," I say humbly, a rueful smile on my lips. "Though I would of course like to thank my dear friends Malala and Michelle Obama for their support and encouragement. I know that I stand upon the shoulders of giants, for truly we are a nation. . ."

"Effie?" Miss Sardana's voice drags me from my daydream.

"Oh, sorry," I say quickly, "could you just repeat that for me?"

Miss Sardana sighs. "I said, we haven't got a bunker, but I *might* be able to help you."

Angelika squeezes my arm.

"It really might not be what you have in mind." Miss Sardana raises a finger in warning.

"That would be very gracious of you," I say in a deeply presidential tone. "Please, lead the way."

Miss Sardana guides us out of her classroom and stops in front of a brown door. She turns the handle and pulls the door open, revealing nothing but darkness beyond. Stepping inside, she fumbles to locate a light switch and a flickering bulb hums to life overhead.

We are standing in what can only be described as a cupboard.

It is pretty big for a cupboard, don't get me wrong, I could easily lie down stretched out on the floor in both directions if I chose to do so, but there is no getting around the fact that there are no windows and it is definitely, undeniably, a cupboard.

"It's a cupboard," Angelika says, once more giving voice to my own innermost thoughts.

Miss Sardana nods. "Yes," she agrees. "But it's an *empty* cupboard. Well, almost." Here she gestures to a load of old but perfectly usable sports equipment that is piled up, gathering dust. "All this needs chucking out now that the football team have bought new equipment." *Obviously these are the Aaron Davis rejects*, I think, fuming. "This stuff is all rather in the way," Miss Sardana concludes glumly, as if moving some bags of balls and cones and hurdles is a simply insurmountable task.

"Not for long," I cry, turning to face them both. "It's perfect. Look, we can fit a table in ... a small one anyway, and put some cushions on the floor. Our meetings will be cool and informal. We'll be like an artsy design company drinking green tea and mind-mapping great ideas. We can cover the walls in posters. We can lock ourselves away and talk for hours about the issues that matter and about how we're going to make the school a better place for everyone, not just a few popular kids." My eyes are shining and as I look around the cupboard I can see the transformation unfolding in my mind. "It's not an empty cupboard any more," I sigh happily. "It's the campaign headquarters for Effie Kostas. And I *am* running for junior class president." My voice goes up at the end, and I pump my fist in the air, dramatically. Angelika bursts into spontaneous applause and I think even Miss Sardana looks quite moved.

"Thanks, miss," I say seriously. "This is the first step in a very important journey."

"It's fine, Effie." Miss Sardana shrugs, already backing away as though she's relieved to have us out of her hair. "Good luck with your campaign."

We are interrupted by the ringing of the bell and so Angelika and I rush off to our maths lesson, but my head is still jangling with the image of the Kostas Campaign HQ and I can't wait for lunchtime to roll around so that we can get back in there.

During the lunch break we drag Jess along to our first official team meeting. She immediately agrees to be part of the campaign team, and admires our new office with some enthusiasm.

"I've got some big purple cushions in my room that will be great for sitting on, I can bring them in," Jess offers.

"Look at all these shelves!" Angelika exclaims, eyeing up the wall of built-in shelving on one side. "We can keep all our supplies in here — stuff for making posters and leaflets and things."

I nod, pleased that they have both immediately seen the potential for the space.

"Are you any good at art, Effie?" Jess asks. "Because I know for a fact that Angelika is rubbish. And I'm not much better. I like maths. Numbers behave themselves much better than words and pictures do."

"No," I say, sadly. "I'm not much good at art either."

"Well then, it's clear – the first thing we need to do is recruit a couple more people for the team," Angelika says.

"Do you think we need more than us three?" I ask doubtfully.

"Definitely." Angelika nods. "We've got a lot of work to do, and not a lot of time to do it. We need to build up your following, get your name out there, so we need someone else who's outgoing and persuasive. And we DEFINITELY need an artist. We're the organizers but we need to make sure we can represent the whole junior school . . . that means getting as many people as possible."

"We aren't going to fit many more people in here," Jess points out. She's right, it's already a bit of a squeeze with three.

"Well, at least a couple more," Angelika says firmly. "We need some people outside of our group. I've got an idea about recruiting the artist –" she taps her cheek thoughtfully "– but we should try and get the word out to other people who are interested in taking down Aaron. There must be lots of us!"

We all agree and we spend the rest of lunch making posters. They look like this:

We leave our cupboard HQ so that we can run around sticking the posters up in the halls. I am carefully pinning one to a noticeboard when I hear a clunking noise beside me. I turn to look and there's an empty plastic water bottle rolling along the floor where it has completely missed the bin. I twirl around to see a boy walking on, his hands in his pockets.

"Oi!" I exclaim. "You've dropped your rubbish on the floor."

The boy turns around to look at me. He has golden curly hair and big blue eyes. He's not much taller than me, but somehow he is giving the impression that he is looking down his nose at me. It's the boy who wouldn't move his backpack in the hall. My blood immediately starts to simmer. "Are you talking to me?" he says, and his voice is quite soft.

"You missed the bin," I reply, pointing to the water bottle. The boy stands beside me and looks down at the bottle with an air of bemusement, as though he's never seen the bottle, the bin or, indeed, this corridor before.

Just then someone else appears around the corner, and I groan under my breath.

"All right, Matt?" Aaron says with a nod. Of course these two equally awful people know each other.

"Yeah, man," the golden boy – Matt – replies.

"Is Kostas giving you trouble?" Aaron asks.

"ME?!" I huff. "Your *friend* is the one who is just throwing his rubbish around in the STREETS."

Aaron looks around in mock confusion. "Hate to

break it to you, Kostas, but we're actually INSIDE at the moment."

Matt snorts, as though Aaron has made an incredibly witty observation, and I treat him to one of my iciest glares, heavily modelled on Lil's deadliest death stare.

"AND," I continue, as though Aaron hasn't spoken, "I can't believe you were going to put that bottle in the bin anyway. This school should have recycling bins. Don't you know that it takes AT LEAST FOUR HUNDRED AND FIFTY YEARS for a plastic bottle to decompose? Or that EVERY DAY, EIGHT MILLION pieces of plastic find their way into our oceans?"

"Whoa, keep your hair on." Aaron holds his hands up in front of him.

"Yeah," Matt chimes in. "Chill out. Why are you being so loud? There's no need to shout."

"I suppose you think KILLING THE EARTH is cool?" I say as cuttingly as possible. "You know, as the school council president, this is EXACTLY the sort of thing you could be doing something about."

"Well, maybe next year, when I'm junior president *again*, I will . . . think about it," Aaron says idly. Then he and Matt wander off together.

"I think that's that weird girl I told you about, the

one who yelled at me before ... who is she?" I hear Matt ask, but I don't hear Aaron's reply.

"I'LL JUST TAKE CARE OF THIS, THEN," I yell after them, scooping up the plastic bottle and stuffing it in my bag to recycle it at home later. I mentally add a decent recycling programme to the list of issues I'll address as president. Actually, this is such a great idea that it makes me feel a little bit better. At least something good is coming out of running into those jerks.

"Was that Matt Spader?" Angelika appears at my elbow.

"Matt someone, yes," I say, and Angelika nods.

"He's one of Aaron's best buddies. Vice captain of the football team," she says.

"Makes sense they'd be friends," I snort. "He seems about as charming as Aaron Davis."

"Hmm." Angelika narrows her eyes. "I bet he'll be Aaron's vice president again if he wins the student council election."

I look at Angelika in dismay. "You mean both of them?" I groan. "They run the council together?"

Angelika nods again. "Yup. The president chooses the vice president so of course Aaron chose Matt ... he's always sucking up to Aaron."

I turn back to the noticeboard and look at our poster. It seems more important every day that I defeat Aaron Davis.

CHAPTER *Ten*

That evening I go round to Angelika's place for tea. Her house is about a ten-minute walk from mine, but unlike our home, which is small and old and wonky, Angelika's is small and new and very square. It is part of a big estate of new houses that all match, lined up neatly on long roads.

Angelika's mum and dad are Polish and they moved to England when Angelika was three, a bit like my yia-yia and papou – they moved here from Greece with my dad when he was the same age and now they live in Manchester. We go up to Angelika's room to watch a film on her laptop. Her mum brings us some little gingerbread biscuits filled with jam and we munch happily as we scroll through Netflix.

Angelika's room looks a bit like mine, but hers is definitely more messy. Her bookshelves are heaving, and I pull down three books to borrow. She says I can keep them as long as I like, and I grin. I think trusting someone with your books is maybe the ultimate sign of friendship.

We sit side by side on the bed with our legs stretched out in front of us and talk about the campaign.

"Do you think anyone else will volunteer?" I ask. "To join the team, I mean."

"I don't see why not," Angelika says, picking up another biscuit. "There are loads of people in the school who would be pleased to see someone challenge Aaron Davis."

"Are there?" I wonder. "He seems pretty popular to me."

"Well, yeah," Angelika says, "but that stuff's just ... pretend, isn't it? Being *popular*? I mean, how many of those people are really Aaron's friends? Real friends, I mean, like us and Jess?"

The way she says it makes me tingle with happiness. I suppose having any friends at all would be a big relief, but having THOSE friends, the two of them, is really special. "I guess you're right," I say slowly, thinking over what she is saying. Also, over the last week things have changed ... when I first decided to run it was so impulsive and all about defeating Aaron. Don't get me wrong, that's still pretty high on my to-do list, but I've started to see real ways that I could make a difference. Raising money for the library, distributing funds to different clubs and societies that aren't run by the cool kids, and a new recycling policy are just the tip of the iceberg.

"I mean, after all, what does Aaron Davis have that I don't have?" I frown. "Apart from nice hair and football skills, I mean."

"I like your hair," Angelika says loyally.

"Thanks," I smile. "But I'm not good at football."

"Wouldn't matter if you were," snorts Angelika. "There's no team for girls."

"WHAT?!" I spring to my feet.

Angelika reaches out to steady the plate of biscuits and looks startled. "There's only a boys' team," she says then. "But why do you care? You just said, you're no good at football."

"It's not about being good at football," I squeak. "It's the principle. Just because I don't really enjoy *playing* football doesn't mean none of the girls in our school do. Has anyone even asked them?"

"Well, no," Angelika admits. "I don't think so."

"There you go," I exclaim. "For all we know the next Steph Houghton might be in our school."

"Who?" Angelika asks.

"She's the captain of the England football team," I say briskly. "Lil's always going on about her. You see, this is all part of the problem. Everyone knows who the male players are even if they don't give a stuff about football. It's totally wrong. My mum says that the women's league is way more fun to watch than the men's." I sit forward now. "Did you know," I say in a low voice, "that during the First World War, when most of the men were away, there was a huge women's football league and it was really popular?"

"What, really?" Angelika asks, surprised.

I nod eagerly. "Yes, at this one match there were over fifty thousand people inside the stadium watching, and thousands and thousands more all shouting outside who wanted to get in. It was a really big deal and then after the war finished everyone got all freaked out about women being just as good at football as men so they BANNED women's teams from the clubs."

"That's terrible," Angelika breathes.

"Exactly," I say. "And that's why this is really

important. All these messages that people send out, even without necessarily meaning to, that boys are better at some things than girls. It's stupid, and Lil loves playing football. When she comes up to Highworth Grange there needs to be a girls' team waiting for her."

Angelika is grinning at me again. "Sounds like someone had better do something about it then," she says.

When I get home that evening I'm still thinking about my conversation with Angelika.

"Did you know there's no girls' football team at Highworth Grange?" I ask my mum and dad.

"I didn't think you liked playing football?" my dad says distractedly.

"Daaaaaad," I groan. "That is *so* not the point."

"Of course it's not," Mum pipes up from beside me on the sofa. "If there's a boys' team then there should be a girls' team."

"Exactly," I agree.

"Hey, I'm not disagreeing." Dad holds up his hands in surrender. "I was just surprised it was something that you were particularly worried about."

I think about that for a second. "Well, I suppose

it's not all about what I want, is it? The point of trying to make a difference is thinking about what everyone else needs too."

Mum and Dad share a little look at this, and a secret smile passes between them. It's the same look they gave each other at Lil's gymnastics tournament, or that time my experiment won first prize at my primary school science fair.

"I think that's absolutely right," Mum says, pulling me into a big hug. Dad comes over and wraps his arms around her so that the three of us are all curled up like a cuddly cinnamon roll with me in the middle.

"Ugh!" Lil's voice interrupts, "Are you three being soppy again?" but Dad reaches out and pulls Lil into the cuddle and when she starts squawking in protest, Mum starts smothering her in noisy kisses, and then the four of us are laughing and laughing and it takes a while to untangle ourselves.

"Oh, Effie, Iris was asking about you," Lil says finally, her cheeks glowing pink. Lil and I have both taken to dropping in on Iris and eating all her biscuits. Lil bullied Iris into watching *Frozen* and now she's undertaken a full education in all things Disney. Iris pretends to put up with it very grumpily, but I caught her humming "A Whole New World" yesterday.

"I'll go over tomorrow," I say, glancing at my watch. "It's a bit late now and I've got to get ready for a big day tomorrow. Actually," I add, slowly, "while you're all here, I have something to tell you."

I pause dramatically to make sure that I have their attention, all three of them sit pleasingly still and quiet, and I feel a bit like the presenter announcing the next winner of *The X Factor*.

"I have decided to run for junior class president on the student council," I blurt out. "There's a campaign and then everyone votes in December. The boy who is president now is sort of the worst and so I've decided to defeat him and lead the school to glory." I wait for them to jump up and tell me how proud they are and how much they support me.

Instead, my mum and dad are suspiciously quiet.

"Cool," Lil says, and at least *she* looks interested. "Will you have bodyguards and a big black car that drives you around with bulletproof windows?"

"Well, no," I say, although the image is a good one. I can just imagine myself in my power suit and my big sunglasses clicking away on my phone in the back, tackling the day-to-day issues of being a political megastar.

"Oh." Lil looks disappointed. "Well, never mind ... I'm sure it will still be good," she says comfortingly, although her voice doesn't sound particularly convinced.

"What do you think?" I ask Mum and Dad.

"I think it's great, Eff," my dad says, rubbing the back of his neck.

"Yes," Mum chimes in, "great." Her voice wavers a bit. "It's only. . ." She trails off here.

"What?" I ask, confused. I thought they'd be really pleased.

"Well, darling," Mum says now, "don't you think that there's enough going on with moving and starting a brand-new school? Shouldn't you be focusing on your schoolwork and settling in, making new friends?"

I can feel my mouth drop open in surprise. "You don't think I should do it?" I ask, stunned. My mum and dad have always been my biggest cheerleaders; usually they're almost embarrassingly encouraging.

"It just seems like a lot to take on," Dad says quickly.

"Yes," Mum jumps in here. "Why not wait a year

until you're a bit more settled before you take on such a big responsibility?"

I gape at them like a particularly simple goldfish. I can't believe that I'm hearing this.

"Just slow things down a bit, eh?" Mum says, reaching for my hand.

I tug my hand away and jump to my feet, trying to think of the most hurtful thing I can, while I whisk out of the room.

"I BET HILLARY CLINTON'S PARENTS NEVER BEHAVED LIKE THIS!" I yell, and I pull the door shut with a satisfying slam and thud upstairs.

CHAPTER *Eleven*

The next day is the day we're hoping our campaign team volunteers will turn up. I am still sulking, and I refuse to talk to Dad as he hands me my dinner money. In my head I have already titled this chapter of my biography: LIKE A PHOENIX RISING FROM THE ASHES: WHEN MY PARENTS LOST FAITH IN ME I ONLY GREW STRONGER. It's a little long I guess. I'll keep working on it. Still, their betrayal has cut me deep. I suppose being a politician means you need to grow a thick skin, but I hadn't expected this kind of behaviour from my own flesh and blood.

"Good news!" Dad exclaims cheerily. "I'm making my famous spanakopita for dinner tonight. Your favourite."

I give him a haughty look which I hope conveys my profound disappointment in his behaviour, but also my weary awareness of his shortcomings.

"Are you all right, Effie?" he asks, startled. "Are you feeling sick? Do you have a headache or something?"

"No," I reply crushingly. "Only a pain in my back from where MY OWN FAMILY STUCK THE KNIFE IN."

"Someone stuck a knife in you?" Lil asks, wide-eyed as she appears in the kitchen doorway. "Can I see?" She's peering at the back of my blazer with barely concealed glee.

If I didn't know better, I would think Dad was trying not to laugh. I glare at him again.

"Metaphorically, Lil," I snap, with a toss of my head as I storm out and head for the front door. "It's a metaphorical knife."

"Oh." I hear Lil's wistful voice as I grab my backpack. "Shame."

When I get to school I tell Angelika about Mum and Dad, and she shrugs and gives a world-weary sigh. "Parents," she says, as if that one word explains everything.

"I suppose," I mutter. I am quiet for a moment.

"But do you think they might have a point? Do you think it's taking on too much to run?" I ask, and my voice is a bit small. "Do you think we can win?" I've checked the list and it turns out that I *am* the only one brave/dumb enough to run against Aaron, and I don't know if that makes things better or worse.

"Why not?" Angelika asks. "Haven't you ever seen a film? You're the underdog, and the underdog always comes from humble beginnings to snatch victory at the end."

"You're right," I say, feeling immediately sunnier. Angelika's confidence is contagious. And after all, we've got lots of time before the election. We just need to make a splash, to win over our fellow students and to show them all the different ways that having a president like me could help to improve the school.

We greet Jess and the three of us make our way through the school gates. Jess has geography, but Angelika and I are going to a history lesson in a different part of the school.

"See you later," Jess calls over her shoulder. "For the big meeting at lunch!"

My stomach does a little flip then. I wonder if anyone will turn up, or if it will just be the three of us sitting in an empty cupboard again. I suppose there's only one way to find out.

"Oh, I've got an idea about that," Angelika says. "We'll have to make a bit of a detour during morning break."

"What for?" I ask.

"You'll see," Angelika says mysteriously.

When morning break rolls around, Angelika doesn't waste any time in dragging me off to the art room.

"We'll definitely find a good artist in here," she says.

There are a few students in the classroom, mostly older kids wearing clompy boots and black eyeliner, but in one corner is a small boy with red hair hunched over a sketchbook. We make a beeline for him.

"Hi," I say.

The boy looks up, his sandy freckles standing out on his pale skin. "H-hello," he says nervously, as though he half expects us to turn him upside down and make off with his dinner money.

I give him what I hope is a reassuring grin and he blinks anxiously at me.

"What's your name?" I ask, sticking out my hand. The boy shakes it tentatively.

"K-Kevin," he manages.

Angelika leans chummily against the table. "Well, Kevin, we're on the lookout for a good artist," she says. "Know anyone who might fit the bill?"

"A good artist?" he repeats faintly.

"Your stuff's pretty good," Angelika says, leaning over to peek at his sketch pad.

Kevin seems to have grasped that it's unlikely we're about to turn into weirdly specific artist bullies, but he still covers his work protectively. "Oh," he says. "Well, thanks. Yeah, I like art."

"And we have need of an artist," Angelika says out the side of her mouth as though she's trying to organize some sort of criminal activity.

Kevin looks alarmed again and I decide to take matters into my own hands. "Hi, Kevin," I smile. "I'm Effie Kostas, and this is my friend Angelika." Angelika gives a little salute. "I'm actually running for junior student council president," I say, "and we were wondering if you'd be interested in helping out with the campaign?" I flash him another glittering smile. "We're looking for someone to make posters and things with a bit of artistic flair."

"Oh." Kevin frowns. "I . . . I see. Well, it's just I'm only in year seven, so I didn't know if you would want me to. . ." He trails off here, casting another nervous glance at Angelika.

"That doesn't matter," I say firmly. "In fact it would be great to have someone from year seven on the team . . . after all, the junior president has to look after all three junior years."

"I suppose," Kevin agrees slowly.

"And I think you're being let down by the current president," I say now, in my best campaigning voice.

"I don't think the current president has much to do with me," Kevin says, and he sounds a bit glum.

"But that's where you're wrong, Kevin!" I exclaim. I glance around the art room. "Why isn't there an art club?" I ask.

"There is," Kevin says. "But not many people come. It's mostly just people sitting in here quietly getting on with their coursework, anyway."

"But what if you had some funding?" I say beadily. "For special materials or trips to exhibitions or to get guest speakers in."

Kevin's eyes are growing starry. "Well, that sounds amazing," he says, "but there's never any money left over for the art club."

My grin stretches even wider. "Until now," I say. "Until now."

When the bell rings for lunch, Angelika and I leap out of our seats and hustle to campaign HQ. Jess is only slightly behind us.

"I wonder if Kevin will turn up," I say anxiously.

"It definitely seemed like you had won him over," Angelika replies.

"Who's Kevin?" Jess asks, and just then I see a blaze of red hair rounding the corner towards us.

"Hi," Kevin says nervously. "I guess this is the right place then."

"You made it!" I exclaim gleefully, and he looks pleased that I'm so pleased.

"I . . . er . . . made this," Kevin says, and he unzips his giant backpack, carefully pulling out a laminated sheet of paper. It's a sign for the front of the door and it says:

in big swirling letters. It's beautiful.

"Wow," Jess says. "That's really good."

I nod in agreement.

"That's so much better than yours, Effie," Jess continues.

"Yes," I agree.

"Yours was just plain embarrassing, compared to this," Jess adds.

"Mmm," I say.

"I mean, it looked like yours was done by a toddler or something. . ."

"Yes, thanks, Jess," I say firmly, cutting her off before she can get any further. From the gleam in her eyes I can tell Jess has plenty more to share about my lack of artistic ability.

With great ceremony we tape the sign to the door, and I feel a bubble of happiness in my chest as I look at it, and at the people standing beside me. It makes me feel full of feelings, like I'm about to pop with it all and spray them in a sort of disgusting cloud of glitter and rainbows and sparkly unicorn dust.

"So," Angelika says brightly. "Shall we go in and wait?"

We go inside and turn the light on. Jess hasn't brought her cushions in yet, but we've dragged in a table and a couple of chairs. Angelika and I perch on the table, our legs swinging. I start mentally running through my plans for the meeting. I really want to make sure everyone has a specific job that will best suit their particular skills, and also to clarify what issues we want to focus on during the campaign. I have a list of possibilities, but as there are seventy-five items on it we may need to narrow it down slightly. The minutes tick by, and we give up making awkward conversation after a while. Jess is humming now, something loud and a bit tuneless.

Finally, finally, just when I am about to give up, there is a very soft knock at the door. It is so soft, in fact, that if we hadn't all been sitting in total silence, I doubt that we would have heard it.

"I'll get it," I cry, leaping to my feet and shoving the door open. Standing on the other side is a girl in a grey Puffa jacket, zipped tight and her hood pulled up so that only a bit of her face is visible. Her hand is still in the air thanks to my speed in

ZO

KEVIN

109

answering her knock. I notice that her fingers are shaking quite badly and that her eyes are wide as she steps back in alarm at my enthusiastic greeting.

"Hi! Hi!" I exclaim, bubbling over with enthusiasm. "Are you here for the campaign team meeting?"

The girl's eyes slide to the side as if she is considering running away, and then she jerks her head into a quick nod.

"Great," I say. "Come on in."

The girl follows me cautiously into the cupboard, standing awkwardly on the threshold as she eyes my three pals.

"I'm Effie," I say now, and I bring my voice down so it's a bit calmer and quieter. It's obvious from the way the girl is standing, hunched into her coat, her hands buried in her pockets and her eyes on the floor in front of her, that she is feeling shy. She is quite big, but the way she stands is as if she wants to make herself so small that she disappears completely.

Fleetingly, her eyes meet mine, and I can see that her cheeks are red. She doesn't say anything.

"This is Angelika, Jess and Kevin," I say, pointing to each of them.

"You're in my maths class," Jess says. "Your name's Zo."

The girl nods again.

"Right," I say brightly. "Well, I suppose we should bring this meeting to order."

CHAPTER *Twelve*

"So," I say, channelling my most presidential voice and clasping my hands behind my back. I begin to stride forward, because I always think pacing seems like the sort of thing important, clever people do, but unfortunately there is nowhere for me to actually stride *to* in this squished room, so I come to an abrupt halt, sort of bouncing off the wall like a character in a computer game. "Um." I clear my throat, swinging back to face them. "Thank you all for coming to this meeting. My name is Effie, and I'm running for junior class president." I pause here and Angelika applauds loudly. After a second the others join in, but a lot less enthusiastically.

"Thank you," I say, raising my hands to silence them. "It really means a lot to me that you all came today. I know that I'm new to this school, but I really do think that the student council is so important, and, as president, there are loads of positive things that I can do to improve this school for everyone."

Angelika nods encouragingly, Jess is staring thoughtfully into the distance, Kevin makes a sort of murmuring noise in the back of his throat, and Zo remains silent. It's not exactly the rapturous response I was hoping for, but I plough on regardless.

"So," I continue, "I suppose the first thing to discuss is different jobs. Obviously, Kevin will be in charge of art and design. Angelika is the campaign manager … although…" I turn to face her. "Are you sure that's not too much with you running for secretary again? Will you have time?"

Angelika waves her hand dismissively. "I'm the only person running," she says, "so the job's already mine. No one wants to be secretary because you have to be super organized and in charge of all the paperwork." Her eyes gleam here. "Which is why I love it."

Once again I reflect on how much of a kindred

spirit Angelika is. Only this morning we had a pretty heated debate over the best kind of paper for making notes on. I said blue-lined, narrow-ruled paper WITH margins because I'm not completely devoid of good common sense, but Angelika favours an unlined notebook. Apparently she's more of a visual thinker and she likes to throw in the odd mind-map so I suppose it sort of adds up, even if she is technically wrong. We might be quite different in some ways, but our shared love of organization and stationery is creating the kind of unbreakable bond that I would usually attribute to my preferred brand of superglue.

"Great," I say, "so that leaves Jess, who I thought might be in charge of communications, gathering support with other students and teachers?" I look over at her questioningly and she nods. "And then there's Zo. . ." I look over at the girl, who shrinks even further back into her coat (if such a thing is possible). "Maybe you can just sort of float and we'll work out where you fit in best later on?" I smile encouragingly at her and she responds with another quick, jerky nod.

"And I guess that means I'm security," a voice cracks from the doorway. Angelika, Kevin and Jess

are all staring over my shoulder with wide eyes; Zo
has retreated so far into the shadows that I don't
know what she's doing. I spin around and then I
can understand everyone's surprise. Even though
I have only been at the school for a short time I
recognize Ruby Frost. A girl from the year above,
she is chewing gum, snapping
it between her teeth, her blazer
jangles with lots of different metal
pin badges and the heels on her
school shoes make her about half
a foot taller than the rest of us.
She's intimidatingly pretty, with
sharp, slanting cheekbones and
glowing dark-brown skin.

"All right?" she says, with
a crack of her pink gum. "Is
this the place for the campaign
meeting?"

"Yes," I manage. "I'm Effie."

"Cool," Ruby says, stalking in
and shaking her long hair, which
is plaited into hundreds of tight
braids.

Jess is looking at her in

bemusement. "What are you doing here?" She asks the question we've all been wondering about in her usual blunt way. Ruby doesn't seem offended.

"I heard about Effie standing up to Aaron in the canteen. Caring is cool," she says with an easy shrug and another snap of her gum. "Everyone knows that. It's about time we had a girl in charge, if you ask me." She grins at me, and I grin back.

"OK, great," I say. "I agree! And I think we should be standing up and making some noise. I'm sick of people telling me to be quiet about the things I care about." There's a ripple of agreement here, and the room seems to relax a bit. Well, apart from Zo, who is still eyeing me warily from deep inside her coat. I flash a reassuring smile at her.

"So, I suppose the first thing to do is to talk about the issues we want to focus on in the campaign," I say, pulling out my list, which covers four sides of A4. "I've jotted down a few ideas, so if we go through the first thirty or so today. . ."

"That sounds really, um, ambitious." Kevin is wide-eyed.

"That list is way too long," Jess says bluntly.

"I know," I sigh, "but there's just so much to do!"

"Why don't you tell us what you think are the top

three or four things?" Angelika suggests.

I gaze at my list, agonized. It's like choosing three scoops in an ice cream shop that serves seventy of your favourite flavours. I make a strangled noise.

Ruby pinches the list from my hands and runs her eyes over it. "This one just says WHALES with a question mark by it. Do you want to get whales for the school? Like a mascot or something? That could be cool."

"No." I shake my head, taking the list back and studying it. I'd written some of these things down quite late at night and my handwriting was a bit messy. "Oh, yes, I know. I was watching this documentary about whales and there's this charity that does conservation work for whales and dolphins. . ."

"A dolphin would be a lot easier to fit in the school than a whale," Jess points out. "Whales are massive."

"No, I don't want us to *adopt* one," I say desperately, "I want us to raise money for them."

"Oh." Jess looks a bit disappointed.

"Well, that's a good idea," Angelika says, "but it's kind of specific and the sort of thing you could do if you win. Maybe for campaigning we just need a couple of big, broad ideas."

I nod eagerly, seeing the sense in what she says. This is why you can't do these things alone. I hand the list around and we get down to discussion. By the time lunch has finished we have a list that we pin on the wall.

MAKE SOME NOISE
– The Effie Kostas Campaign Issues –

★ **REDUCE, REUSE, RECYCLE:**
Get the school to be greener and start a proper recycling campaign.

★ **CLUBS FOR ALL:**
Make more funding available for people who want to start their own clubs and societies NOT JUST THE BOYS' SPORTS TEAMS.

★ **NO ONE EATS ALONE:**
Set up a buddy system so that no one feels left out. Introduce mentors for new students so that they feel welcome and included.

★ **WE NEED LIBRARIES:**
Raise funds for new books and a proper librarian. Libraries aren't a luxury, we need them.

★ ~~Maybe still look into getting a dolphin though?~~

When I walk home later that afternoon it is with a spring in my step that would rival Tigger at his most bouncy. I have a team behind me, and I feel certain that together we can succeed. I mean, yes, we're a bit of an odd bunch, but I just feel it in my bones that we are going to do great things. As I get closer to home, however, my mood takes a dive. In all the excitement I had forgotten about the ruthless betrayal of my so-called "parents". I decide to put off dealing with them by dropping in to see Iris.

She is not sitting on her doorstep and so I ring the doorbell, hearing the echo of it tinkling inside. There is a long pause as Iris shuffles through to answer it.

"Oh," she says when she sees me, "it's you." Which I've come to realize is Iris code for "I'm really happy to see you".

"I suppose you'd better come in," she calls over her shoulder, already moving through to the kitchen.

"Hello, Lennon," I call cheerfully as I bundle into the lovely warm kitchen. Lennon is out of his cage, stretching his wings, and is currently perched on the back of a chair. It smells of cake in here and I notice with interest that Iris seems to have been baking.

"AWFUL CRONE!" Lennon croaks.

"Gosh, thanks," I say, going over to offer him a nut

out of the jar that Iris keeps on the side for him. "We really need to work on your manners."

"Don't you go trying to fix my parrot," Iris snaps. "I like him just as he is."

"USELESS TURNIP!" Lennon shrieks.

"That's right, my lovely," Iris croons. "You tell her." Lennon whistles and bobs his head.

I settle into my seat and I'm thrilled when Iris deposits a slab of fruit cake in front of me.

"This looks great," I say, digging straight in. The cake is still warm and it's sweet and a bit spicy with crunchy brown sugar on top. "Oh wow, this is so good!"

Iris sniffs, but I can tell that she's pleased even when she tries to hide it. "Well, don't get used to it," she says sharply. "I'm not going to be baking for you all the time now. Custard creams are plenty good enough for you and your sister."

"What are you and Lil watching next?" I ask, spraying crumbs everywhere, which I hastily try and clean up.

"Something about an emperor," Iris says, lowering herself into her seat with a sigh. Iris can't be on her feet too long. I guess that's why she doesn't seem to leave the house very much. I've noticed that there's a wheelchair by the front door, but it's mostly buried under a load of coats and scarves.

"*The Emperor's New Groove*!" I exclaim. "That's my favourite. That or *Mulan*. It's a tough one."

"Hmmm," Iris grumbles. "Lot of nonsense if you ask me. Although things do seem to have moved on from *Snow White*, I'll grant you."

"Well, I think you'll enjoy them," I say.

"Not got much choice, with the way your sister bosses me around." Iris tries to look grumpy, but her eyes are soft and crinkled at the corners.

I choose not to answer that and hide a smile behind my hand, stuffing another piece of delicious cake in my mouth. Today has been a good day. No doubt about it, things are definitely looking up.

CHAPTER *Thirteen*

I should have known it wouldn't last. Everything begins well enough, and the next day we have another campaign meeting during the lunch break.

We've been in the cupboard for about fifteen minutes, and I'm relieved to see that everyone has come back again ... even Zo, who sticks to her favourite shadowy corner.

I mention my idea about the girls' football team and Ruby lights up. "Oh, wicked," she says. "I love football. I'm way better than my brothers. I'd love it if there was a team I could join."

"That could be really good for your campaign, too," Angelika says thoughtfully. "After all, it's a matter of equality and fairness . . . which is what your run for president is all about."

There's a warm feeling in my chest. Seeing someone be so enthusiastic about one of my ideas, seeing the way those ideas could actually make a difference to a real person . . . well, that's definitely exciting. Ruby and I agree to talk more about next possible steps together.

"Right, so I asked Miss Sardana about the debate," I say, moving on to the next item on my list, "but she had to check with Ms Shaarawi, because apparently they haven't even HAD the debate part of the campaign for YEARS." I roll my eyes. "What is the point of laying out the rules of the election if they're not going to follow them?"

"I think last year no one bothered to run against Aaron," Jess points out. "Would have been a bit weird if he had been up on stage debating with himself."

"Quite funny, though," Ruby snorts from the purple cushions on the floor where she is sprawled. "He could have run from one side of the stage to the other and back again."

"He could have worn a wig," Kevin ventures, getting into the spirit of things. "Or one of those costumes where one half of him looks like one person, and the other looks like someone else so he has to keep turning from side to side?"

"Oooh, yeah," Ruby agrees. "*That* would be worth watching. Good one, Kev."

Kevin flushes with pleasure at having won Ruby's approval.

"Well, as much as we would ALL enjoy watching Aaron Davis arguing with himself, this year he'll be arguing with ME," I say. "And losing," I add firmly.

"Too right!" Ruby calls.

"So when is the debate being held?" Jess asks, her pen in her hand to make a note in the OFFICIAL campaign diary that Angelika provided.

"It's on the twelfth of December," I say with a little shiver. "The day before the election."

"Right," Angelika puts in. "So we've got lots of time left to prepare for that. And the student fair is in a couple of weeks."

I frown, crinkling my forehead. "I've never been to one before, so what do people usually do?" I ask.

"Well, we need to book a stand," Angelika says. "People sell stuff to raise money for the school – cakes and biscuits and things usually. We decorate the stand with a theme that reflects something about our campaign and we all dress up, and there's a prize for the best decorations."

"The band usually play and people sing or dance on the stage as well," Jess explains. "And parents come as well as students."

"Yeah, 'cos they're the ones that splash out the cash on wonky gingerbread men." Ruby snorts.

"OK," I say, although I don't really want to think about my parents at the moment . . . two days after our disagreement and things are still pretty frosty between us. Dad keeps casting me mournful glances and sighing heavily while I answer all his questions in monosyllables. "So we've got a while, but we also need to start thinking about themes for that. Something that sums up all that we're about and hope to accomplish," I finish briskly.

The team nods.

"So, can we go and get some lunch now?" Ruby asks, clutching her stomach. "I'm starving."

"Yes," I agree. "Meeting adjourned."

While everyone stands and gathers their bags I look down at my notebook.

"Are you coming?" Angelika asks from the door.

"I'll be right behind you," I say. "I just want to

make sure that I've got everything down before it all goes out of my head."

"OK," Angelika grins. "I'll save you a piece of chocolate cake."

"Thanks," I breathe, gratefully.

I take a moment in the quiet solitude of my cupboard office to look through my notes, and I feel a tingle of satisfaction at how official they look.

When I leave I close the door carefully behind me and then I turn to find myself confronting Matt Spader.

"Hello," he says in his soft voice.

"Oh, hello," I say briskly.

"I'm glad I bumped into you." He waves a hand in the air. "I wanted to say sorry about the other day."

"Oh?" I am thrown.

"Yeah." He shrugs. "You were right about the recycling thing. It was a good idea." The words coming out of his mouth are friendly enough but something seems off to me.

"I know it was a good idea," I say suspiciously.

His smile widens even further. "Look," he says, "I just think someone should tell you, in a nice way, that this campaign thing isn't going to work out for you."

"Right," I grind out, my suspicions confirmed – this isn't a friendly chat at all. "And why is that?"

"I'm not trying to be mean or anything," he says earnestly. "It's just that you're wasting your time. Aaron's definitely going to win. There's nothing you can do about it, so you might as well stop now. I'm doing you a favour by saying this. You're new and you don't get how things work yet." He gives a little laugh and that smile again. "I just don't want you to look like an idiot."

I stare at him for a second, my mouth hanging open. My brain is buzzing, full of white noise. I'm so surprised that I can't even seem to grasp at a fitting retort.

"I'm just trying to be friendly," Matt says in a very over the top *kind* voice.

"FRIENDLY?" I snap. "Telling me I'm making an idiot of myself? Why shouldn't I run if I want to? Isn't it for all the other students to decide if Aaron's 'DEFINITELY' going to win or not?" I make exaggerated air quotes, just to really make it clear that I am not at all convinced by his rubbish argument.

Matt purses his lips, like he's bitten into a lemon. "There's no need to get hysterical about it," he huffs. "I'm just trying to do the right thing. If you want to make yourself look stupid then that's your business."

"I am NOT hysterical," I bite out. "I am ANGRY. And the only person who looks stupid right now is

YOU because you're completely underestimating me AND the rest of the students here."

Matt sighs in a put-upon way and runs his hand through his golden locks. "Well, I'm sorry you feel like that," he says. "You really don't see that you haven't got a chance, do you?" He shakes his head pityingly. "Don't say I didn't warn you." And then he saunters off, leaving me behind, staring after him and thinking of a hundred clever things I could have said.

"And then he said he was trying to be FRIENDLY," I groan later, over a cup of tea at Iris's kitchen table.

"WHAT A MORON," Lennon howls.

"You've never been more right, Lennon," I sigh.

"Sounds to me like Aaron's worried you might actually be competition," Iris says, looking at me over the top of her mug.

"Do you think?" I ask softly. I can't shake the queasy butterfly feeling that's been in my stomach since the encounter with Matt. "You don't think. . ." I trail off. "You don't think. . ." I try again.

"Spit it out," Iris demands.

"You don't think he might be right, do you?" I ask finally, and my voice is hardly more than a whisper.

"What if I am just making a fool of myself?" I sink into my chair.

Iris eyes me beadily. There's not a trace of sympathy in her face. "Standing up for what you believe in is never foolish," is all she says.

I sigh. I know she's right, but I can't help hearing Matt's voice again in my head. I hate that he's made me doubt myself.

"You know, Effie," Iris says finally, "I can see a lot of myself in you."

"Can you?" I ask, surprised.

"Oh yes." Iris nods. "But of course you have opportunities that I could only have dreamed of. It's exactly the sort of thing the rest of us have been fighting for all these years. So that young girls like you can dream of growing up to be prime minister." Iris gestures crossly towards a pile of papers on the table. "These days all I can do is write letters to people, but back in the day I used to march and protest with the best of them." She lifts her chin, proudly, her pink hair gleaming in the afternoon sunlight filtering through the window.

"Really?" I ask, immediately intrigued. "What was it like? What did you march for?"

A grin spreads across Iris's face, scrunching it up

and making her look much younger than usual. "Oh yes," she says. "It was wonderful. You've got to try and make your voice heard... no good sitting on your hands and not mucking in. Nothing will ever change that way. If I could still get around like I used to I'd be out there pounding the pavements and making some noise, I can tell you." She reaches for a biscuit. "Actually, my mother marched in the Peace Pilgrimage when she was pregnant with me, in the summer of 1926, so I didn't really have a choice; protesting was in my blood."

"1926," I goggle. That is a seriously long time ago. I do the maths in my head. Iris must be over ninety, which is even older than I thought. I think about all the things she's seen and how much has changed since then.

She takes a slurp of her tea. "Yes," she says now. "Women from all over Britain marched miles and miles to London, carrying flags and chanting to try and get the government to talk about peace instead of getting themselves ready for war... Well —" she grimaces into her cup "— we all know how that turned out. But I consider that my very first protest."

I take this in for a second. If I close my eyes I can almost imagine all the women marching together.

It's amazing to think that Iris's mum saw all these things. I know it's going to sound a bit dim, but I never really think of old people having lived through actual HISTORY, you know? It's like the stuff we learn about at school is so far in the past, it's hard to remember that there are people, *literally living next door to us*, who were actually there.

"That's seriously cool," I say.

"Yes," Iris agrees, looking closely at my face. "It really is." She turns in her chair. "That big box over there," she says. "Go and grab it." She points to a large cardboard box in the corner of the kitchen.

I go over and heave the box on to the big kitchen table. It's bulky but it's not too heavy.

Iris reaches over and pulls the lid off the top with a flourish. Inside the box are lots of bits of paper. Newspaper clippings and magazine articles mostly. There are other things too, leaflets and posters. Lots of them feel old and fragile. I pull a piece of paper out. It is slightly yellow now and covered in bold writing. It says "Women's Weekend Programme" at the top, and it is a list of events with titles like "Women and the Economy" and "Women and Revolution".

"That is from the Women's Liberation Movement conference," Iris says, her fingers stretching out to brush the piece of paper. "It was a long time ago now, in 1970 ... almost fifty years, but it feels like yesterday."

"What was it?" I ask.

"It was a great big meeting where women came together to talk about equality," Iris says. "They hoped they might get up to three hundred women attending but there were almost six hundred of us there in Oxford, and we had big discussions about all sorts of things affecting women – education, job opportunities, equal pay, women in prisons, women in poverty. Oh, such important things." Iris's eyes are shining now. "It was wonderful, Effie, all those women in one place, thinking and talking. It felt like being part of something so big and important."

I feel a shiver running through me. I try and imagine what it must have been like for Iris. I think I know what she means ... at least a little bit. I want to run for student council so that I can make a difference, and when we had our meeting today and everyone got all enthusiastic and we were laughing and sharing ideas it started to feel like something better than just me by myself, like I was a piece in a jigsaw puzzle, fitting in perfectly, making something bigger. It's a good feeling and I'm not about to give it up ... not for Matt Spader, not for Aaron Davis, not for anyone.

PART TWO

The Campaign

CHAPTER *Fourteen*

"Are you sure about this?" I ask Angelika again, tugging at the strap on my shoulder.

"It's going to be great," Angelika replies firmly.

It's the start of a new school week and we are standing outside the front gates to the school, preparing for the launch of the EFFIE KOSTAS FOR PRESIDENT campaign. In the end we decided to appeal to students the old-fashioned way – through their stomachs. So we are handing out cookies while wearing sandwich boards. At first I hadn't known what Angelika meant by sandwich boards, but they're just two big pieces of cardboard tied together by string that hang over your shoulders so you have one board on your front and one on your back ...

making you the middle of the sandwich, I guess. In the pictures that Iris showed me of her mum and her fellow suffragists they actually used them a lot. The grainy pictures show women in long dresses wearing big signs that say VOTES FOR WOMEN. My own campaign team have gone for some slightly more ... *creative* slogans.

My board is keeping things pretty simple. Lil helped me make it and it is very bright and sparkly, with VOTE FOR EFFIE written on each side.

Angelika's board says CAPTAIN AMERICA WOULD VOTE FOR EFFIE and is covered in a collage of pictures of Chris Evans looking brave and handsome. It must have taken her a long time to collect SO many pictures, but I decide not to question this. If Angelika has a shoebox full of pictures of Chris Evans's head, then that's her business.

Jess's board says IF YOU VOTE FOR EFFIE THEN YOU INCREASE HER CHANCE OF WINNING BY A SMALL PERCENTAGE. Jess is, after all, a pretty literal person, and she said she was nervous of making false promises to the voters. She values honesty, and I respect that.

Ruby's board says BIG HAIR, SHOWS SHE CARES! VOTE FOR EFFIE! And then on the back it says OR OTHERWISE YOU'LL HAVE ME TO DEAL WITH. I'm not sure that threatening people is the way to go, but Ruby just laughs and winks at me knowingly. "Sure thing, boss," she says to me as though we are in the mafia. "We're definitely NOT going to threaten anyone. Definitely NOT." I feel a little alarmed and make a mental note to keep an eye on her, make sure she doesn't start saying things about people sleeping with the fishes.

Kevin's board says NOT JUST PEANUTS. I have to admit that I find this one a bit confusing, but he tells me that he looked up successful campaign slogans online and that this one won Jimmy Carter the American presidency, so if it's good enough for him I guess it's good enough for me. "Although," Kevin says thoughtfully, "I think he might have been a peanut farmer so that would make more sense." He thinks this over for a moment. "But if anyone asks, you could just say that you really like peanuts."

Zo doesn't have a board, but she's here, still buried deep inside her Puffa jacket, and that's something. Zo sometimes reminds me of our old neighbour's cat who disappeared for a couple of weeks and came back all thin and nervous and jumpy. She hasn't said a word in the last week, but she's turned up to every meeting so she must think it's a worthwhile cause.

The cookies that Kevin has brought with him are a bit of a funny colour and they don't exactly look the most appetizing, but we're committed to the plan so I plaster on a big smile and stride forward to approach my first target, a rather startled-looking year seven. "Hi!" I cry, brightly. "I'm Effie Kostas and I hope you'll consider voting for me for junior class president! Would you like a biscuit?" I rattle the tin under her nose. All I earn in response is a rather rabbity squeak of terror as she dodges past me.

"What was wrong with that?" I frown.

"I think your smile was maybe a bit ... axe-murdery," Jess says.

Ruby nods in agreement. "Yeah," she says. "Just try and be a bit more casual. Like this." She turns and spies a boy I recognize from a few of my classes.

"OI!" Ruby bellows. "YOU!" The boy almost drops his PE kit. "You're going to vote for Effie, right?"

"Oh," the boy stutters. "Er, well, I ... I actually thought maybe Aaron, but, um, maybe ... I ..." He trails off helplessly.

Ruby glares at him in silence.

"Gnnnaaarrr." The boy makes a curious, strangled noise. I take pity on him.

"You should vote for whoever you like," I say. "But I hope you'll keep an open mind and listen to all the candidates before you decide. Would you like a biscuit?" I offer him the tin and he accepts gratefully, pulling out a biscuit and stuffing it into his mouth. His face takes on a strange expression, and he struggles to swallow, his eyes wide and his nose scrunched up.

"Guuuh, thanks," he gasps, finally, backing swiftly away and casting a look of alarm at the biscuit tin. Weird.

"Looks like it's going really well," a familiar voice says from behind me, and I spin around to find myself looking into the handsome, smirky face of Aaron Davis.

"Yes, it's going great, thanks," I say quickly. "Would you like a biscuit?" I am determined to be poised and gracious.

Aaron peers into the tin and then grimaces. "I think I'll give them a miss. They look like someone threw up on them."

Seems like I'm the only one who is trying to keep things polite.

"Well, that's up to you, I suppose," I say sweetly. "How is your campaign going?"

Aaron bares his teeth in a smile. "It's going really great," he says. "Watch."

He turns and catches the arm of a boy who is rushing past. "All right, mate," he says, and the two do a complicated handshake that involves a high five and a fist bump and several sound effects. "Got your vote for the student council thing, right?"

"Yeah, course," the boy says.

Aaron shrugs. "See you at Taylor's house on Thursday?" he asks.

"Yeah, man. See you there," the boy calls over his shoulder.

Aaron turns to me. "Well, that was pretty tough."

My mouth is hanging open. "The. Student. Council. Thing?" I repeat dangerously, and my voice is getting quite squeaky.

"Calm down, Kostas," Aaron says, sticking his fingers in his ears. "You're going to burst someone's eardrum if you carry on at a pitch only dogs can hear."

"You don't even care!" I exclaim, throwing my hands in the air. "Why are you running at all?"

"Well." Aaron purses his lips thoughtfully. "That lunch pass is pretty handy."

"Gahhh!" I splutter, wordlessly. Aaron's grin stretches wider and wider, showing off so many teeth that he looks like a shark. I recover a bit of dignity and draw myself up in front of him. "Well," I say finally, "we'll see how that argument goes down at the student debate, won't we?"

For the first time Aaron looks a bit confused. "What debate?" he asks.

"Ohhhh," I exhale. "You haven't looked up the rules of the election yet, have you?"

Aaron doesn't reply but his silence says it all.

"Well, you and I are going to have a debate," I say gleefully. "A real one. And then you're going to look like an idiot if you haven't got anything to say about the issues that matter."

Something flickers in his eyes, just for a second. It might be anger or worry, I can't tell. "You're the one who's going to look like an idiot," is all he says. "It'll be five minutes of saying how great the school is and it's all over. No one wants to hear your boring speeches."

My mouth is hanging open again. "But that's ridiculous!" I exclaim. "That's not a proper debate!"

Aaron gives another shrug. "Anyway, good luck

with your little *campaign*." He moves his fingers in air quotes around the word.

I look over at my team, who are enthusiastically pouncing on incoming students, pressing biscuits on them and singing my praises. I feel something glowing in my chest that makes me lift my chin stubbornly.

"Good luck to *you*," I say firmly. "You're going to need it."

Aaron treats me to another smirk and strides off into the school.

I chat with another three or four students, offering biscuits and trying not to smile like an axe murderer, then I find myself face-to-face with our head teacher, Ms Shaarawi.

"Hello, Effie," she says.

"Hello, miss," I beam, surprised that she knows my name. Word of my excellent campaigning must be spreading like wildfire already. "Would you like a biscuit?"

"No, I won't, thank you," Ms Shaarawi says. "And I'm afraid I'm going to have to ask you to stop giving biscuits out to the other students."

"Oh." I am puzzled. "Why?" I can feel my cheeks turning pink as the feeling that I'm in trouble for something creeps in.

"We can't give out food to students like this because many of them have allergies and we can't be sure exactly what's in these." She gestures to the tin in my hand.

"Oh, there's no need to worry, miss," Kevin cuts in, brightly. "My mum's really into health food at the moment so the biscuits don't have any sugar or dairy or gluten in them."

I look down at the tin, aghast. Suddenly their peculiar appearance makes a lot more sense. "What IS in them, Kevin?" I ask weakly.

He tips his head to one side. "Um, I can't remember." He squints thoughtfully. "Avocado, I think. And maybe some chickpeas. Are chickpeas gluten-free?"

Ms Shaarawi is eyeing the biscuits with a queasy look. "Right, well, that's very thoughtful, Kevin, but I still think we might be better off calling a halt to the biscuit distribution."

"So do I!" Jess yells loudly. "They sound absolutely gross!"

"I think they sound really interesting," I say quickly, as Kevin looks crestfallen. "But I suppose rules are rules. So unfair!" I exclaim dramatically. Kevin looks a bit cheered up by this, and I swiftly gather the remaining biscuits to be disposed of. Carefully. Maybe by men in hazmat suits.

"Actually, miss," I say to Ms Shaarawi. "While you're here … there's something I would like to discuss with you…"

CHAPTER *Fifteen*

Emergency Highworth Grange School Council Meeting – Monday 7 November

Minutes recorded by Angelika Lisowski

Meeting called to order at 3.30 p.m. by meeting chair Miss Sardana.

Members present:

Chair Miss Sardana
Aaron Davis (junior student president) (FOR NOW)

Matt Spader (junior student vice president)
Angelika Lisowski (junior student secretary)
Luna Stanworth (junior student treasurer)
Effie Kostas (candidate)

Reading of Agenda

- Miss Sardana explains that meeting has been called at the request of Effie Kostas. There is huffing noise from Aaron Davis. Effie explains emergency meeting called over lack of clarity of student council debate day proceedings.
- Miss Sardana agrees the agenda.

New Business

- Effie Kostas makes passionate speech about the upcoming student president debates. She is a very good public speaker actually. Some might say that she'd make an excellent president. Not me, of course, because I'm just an impartial observer, definitely not a member of her campaign team.
- Effie is banging her hand on the table.

Even I can't write quickly enough to keep up with what she is saying because she has such passion. In short: she wants the student council debate rules to be clearly established, but she also says some very stirring things about a revolution that is brewing and how we should not ignore the downtrodden masses and now she is quoting *Hamilton* lyrics and I'm not sure if she's going to rap or not but I would fully support her if she did.

- She doesn't. :(
- Aaron Davis says that everyone will find the student council speeches boring and that making them longer will just put people off, which is a bit daft if you ask me. Not that I have a strong opinion either way.
- Matt Spader agrees with Aaron.
- Effie Kostas replies that she understands why people find Aaron boring but that she has a lot of interesting things to say.
- Miss Sardana makes a strangled sort of groaning sound and tells them to be quiet. Both candidates are now silent and glowering.
- Luna Stanworth reminds everyone that she

has to get to netball practice.

- Effie takes a deep breath. She is talking slower now so I can catch the details. She wants each candidate to get ten minutes to make their campaign speeches and then for there to be a quick-fire section where candidates have to answer a range of questions on various different topics.

- Snorting sound from Aaron as he asks what she is going to bore on about for ten minutes. Rude.

- Matt Spader laughs hysterically as though Aaron has made a hilarious joke.

- There is a humongous thud as Effie Kostas produces a spectacular ring binder. (Note to self: ask Effie where she got that beast from.) It is stuffed full of paper and has many dividers and Post-it notes sticking out of it. On the front is a picture of her face Photoshopped on to Emmeline Pankhurst's body. She asks if she should go through her issues alphabetically or in order of importance.

- Miss Sardana nervously reminds Effie that we only have the room for ten more minutes.

- Luna Stanworth reminds everyone that she has to get to netball practice.
- Aaron wonders why Effie wants to change everything when "our school is already the best". I, an impartial observer, would not roll my eyes at this kind of laziness, but I wouldn't discourage anyone else from doing so.
- Effie rolls her eyes.
- Matt Spader agrees with Aaron.
- Luna Stanworth reminds everyone that she has to get to netball practice.
- Aaron glares across the table at Effie.
- Matt glares across the table at Effie.
- Effie glares back at both of them.
- Miss Sardana calls for a vote.
- Motion from Effie Kostas: To increase the campaign speech time limit to ten minutes and to alter the remaining layout of the debate to match her suggestions. Vote: Motion carried 4–2.
- Luna Stanworth leaves for netball practice.

Meeting adjourned at 4.00 p.m.

CHAPTER *Sixteen*

It is a cold, wet Tuesday afternoon. Not exactly the most inspirational time to be thinking about playing sports outside, if you ask me, but still, we can't let the weather deter us from our next step on the campaign trail. Ruby and I have agreed on a sort of plan for getting the girls' football team off the ground and it's time to put it into action. I think this is just the sort of thing that will get people talking about our campaign, and I'm hoping it will show that we're going to be a force for good in the school.

After school seems as good a time as any to approach Mrs Gregory, the PE teacher. Ruby and I track her down at the end of the day.

"A girls' football team?" She seems surprised.

"We've never really had any interest in it. Maybe you'd like to sign up for netball instead?"

"No." I shake my head stubbornly. "I don't understand why there's a boys' team but no girls' team."

"It would be cool, miss," Ruby puts in here, "if we could play matches against other schools? Be part of a league?"

"But there isn't is a local girls' league," Mrs Gregory says. "Besides which, we don't have the resources or funding for a team. I'm sorry, girls."

"But maybe we could raise money. We might be able to start a league," I say quickly, "if we start with a team here. All leagues must have to begin somewhere."

Mrs Gregory doesn't look convinced. "Well, yes, I suppose," she says reluctantly. "But with the best will in the world, you can't just magic up a league." She shakes her head. "I'm sorry, girls, it's just too much to take on."

"But I already checked the schedule and at the moment the football pitch is free after school on Thursdays," I persist, grinning at her winningly.

"But I coach the netball team then, Effie." Mrs Gregory is starting to sound impatient now. "I'm afraid I couldn't be there."

"What if we found someone to coach the team?" I jump in. "A parent or something?"

"Yeah." Ruby nods eagerly. "My dad might do it."

Mrs Gregory looks at us for a moment and sighs. "Well," she says finally. "I guess it's a nice idea. If you can get someone to agree to coach, and if you can sign up enough girls . . . maybe twelve to start with, then I will sign off on you using the pitch . . . but, girls, I wouldn't hold your breath. I don't want you to get your hopes up too high."

"Thanks, miss!" we chorus, and then we rush out, flushed with success, and we perform our own improvised victory handshake.

"Do you really think we'll get enough people signed up?" Ruby asks.

"Of course," I say certainly. "We'll set up a sign-up table in the canteen at lunch tomorrow and I bet we'll get loads of interest."

"Yeah." Ruby is enthusiastic. "I feel so FIRED UP! Like I could take on the whole world and win! We could be the start of something for loads of girls."

I beam at her, feeling myself pulled along by a surge of enthusiasm as well. "It will be brilliant."

*

The next day I am feeling a little less optimistic. It's proving harder than I thought to get girls to sign up for our team, especially because lots of the "sporty" girls are already on the netball team. So far we have been here for forty-five minutes and we only have three names.

The real problem is that all three of the girls who have written their names down are really enthusiastic about the idea.

"I've always wanted to be part of a girls' team," one of the girls, who is called Becca, says. "I don't know why I never thought of trying to get a group together myself." She shrugs. "It's so cool that you're doing it."

Hearing things like that feels really good, but it's also a lot of pressure. Now there are girls who will actually be disappointed if we can't make it happen.

"Do you want to sign up for a girls' football team?" I call to a girl who is in my maths class. I wave the clipboard enthusiastically, but she sails straight past as though I haven't spoken.

"I'm really sorry, Ruby," I say glumly. "I thought this bit would be easy."

"Don't worry," Ruby replies, tossing her braids over her shoulder. "We'll get more people. OI!" she shouts at an unsuspecting year seven. "YOU

INTERESTED IN FOOTBALL?" The girl freezes like a rabbit in headlights and makes a squeaking noise before edging silently away.

A shadow looms over our desk and I look up, about to start my pitch for the football team when instead of a prospective teammate, I am confronted by the figure of Aaron Davis. I have never had a nemesis before, but truly Aaron Davis feels like he fits the bill. He's the Joker to my Batman, the Voldemort to my Harry, the Gaston to my Belle.

"What do you want?" I growl.

Aaron picks up the clipboard and looks it over. "Didn't take you for a footballer," he says, his eyebrows raised.

"I'm not," I snap, and I don't know why but it feels like he's just insulted me terribly.

He looks at me, a frown of confusion appearing between his eyes. "So if you don't play football, why are you trying to start a girls' football team?"

"You wouldn't understand," I reply, snatching the clipboard back and placing it neatly on the table in front of me.

"Well, no, I don't," Aaron says. "It seems like you're just getting all worked up over nothing. Why are you making this a big deal? We've never had a girls' team before and nobody cared."

"You mean *you* didn't care," I say, my hair quivering, and I'm starting to worry that it might get so big and angry that it actually throttles him. "What if there wasn't a boys' team? Would you care then?"

"But there isn't a boys' netball team," Aaron points out, "and you don't see the boys getting all upset about it."

"Well, maybe they should be." I find I have jumped to my feet and I'm pointing my finger at him. "Boys should be allowed to play netball if they want, just like girls should be allowed to play football. That's what equality is all about."

"But what if boys don't want to play netball?" Aaron asks, pushing a hand through his hair.

"Why wouldn't they?" I say quickly. "Netball is fun, it's hard work, you have to be skilled to play it. If boys don't play it, it's because they've been told that they shouldn't want to."

"It's a girls' sport," one of Aaron's Neanderthal friends pipes up, appearing at his shoulder. I think his name is Luke. He's like the king of the baboon squad. "No boy wants to play girls' sports. It's embarrassing."

"But why?" I ask, taking a deep breath to try and

remain calm. "Ask yourself why. Why is it so bad for a boy to play a girls' sport? Why do we separate things like that into girls and boys?"

"I dunno." Luke shrugs. "Probably because girls can't play sports like football very well. It's like science or something. You're not fast enough. You don't have the stamina or the strength. Look at your arms . . . so weak. Puny." Here, he flexes a beefy arm and I battle the urge to punch him in the face and show him just how puny my arms are.

"Well, I think there are a load of INSANELY brilliant women footballers who could kick your stupid bum, Luke Travers," Ruby snaps. "Including me, probably."

"You?" Luke snorts. "Not likely."

"Yeah me," Ruby retorts. "Unlike you, my strike rate isn't a total embarrassment."

Luke's face reddens at this. "You don't know what you're talking about. Anyway, I don't know why we're even arguing about it. Things should just stay as they are. The girls have their sports and we have ours. Why can't you just leave things alone? Just . . . you know . . . pipe down, yeah?"

"Just. Stop. Telling. Me. To. Be. Quiet." I grind out. "I am SICK of you and your friends telling me to *pipe down*, or *chill out*, or *stop being so loud*. And anyway, I think that's rubbish." I fold my arms across my chest, where righteous anger is whistling away like a boiling kettle. "It's not fair to boys OR girls. It's like saying there's only one way to be a boy and one way to be a girl. If a boy wanted to play netball, then he'd be called a girl LIKE IT WAS AN INSULT. Like the worst thing a boy could be is like a girl. You just said it would be EMBARRASSING. And when you say things like that then what are you really saying you think about girls? That they're somehow worse? That being like a girl is bad?"

Luke rolls his eyes. "That's stupid," he says.

"I don't know what to say to that," I sit back down, wearily. "It's not an intelligent argument."

"But why are *you* starting a girls' football team if you don't like playing football?" Aaron asks again now. He's been quiet while Luke was arguing with me and Ruby, his eyes moving between us.

I look at him. "Because being a good president isn't about just doing things for yourself," I say. I lift the list and wave it at him. "Whatever you say, there *are* girls in this school who want to do this and at the moment they can't. I think that's wrong and so I want to do something about it. Even if that means sitting here every lunchtime for a week." I slam the clipboard on to the table defiantly. "And you'd understand that if you weren't such a complete and utter Slytherin."

Aaron looks at me for a moment, and I don't know what he's thinking. That little line has appeared again between his eyes. He looks a bit surprised, like that wasn't the answer he expected. He rubs his nose thoughtfully.

"Just leave her, mate," Luke says, tugging at his arm. "She's a psycho."

I glare at him and stick out my tongue. It's not my most mature, sensible argument, but I can't help it.

Aaron shrugs and turns to leave. "Oh, and just for your information," he calls back over his shoulder, into my disbelieving face, "I'm actually not a Slytherin. I'm a Ravenclaw."

CHAPTER *Seventeen*

I trudge home, still annoyed by the scene in the canteen. I mean, some people are still really living in the dark ages. How can we possibly leave the future of our school in the hands of an ignoramus like Aaron Davis? *Ravenclaw*, I snort. *In his dreams.* When I turn my key in the lock on our front door a little later the house is strangely quiet. Not that I really care. Since the INCIDENT in which my family WOUNDED me with their thoughtless DISREGARD of my hopes and dreams, we haven't been making an awful lot of conversation. The only person who seems to be enjoying the atmosphere in our house is Lil, who remarked yesterday that she'd never had so much peace and quiet as she gleefully sat eating Skittles and watching back-to-back recordings of her programmes in what she referred to as "blissful silence".

"I'm home," I call out carelessly now, about to stomp straight up to my room.

"Through here." I hear my mum's voice from the living room. Dumping my bag, I sigh elaborately and make my way inside.

"SURPRISE!" three loud voices shout, making me jump so hard that I almost fall over.

What I see makes a huge, cheek-aching grin spread across my face.

My mum, dad and Lil are all wearing matching white T-shirts with VOTE FOR EFFIE written on them in purple glittery pen. Behind them, a big banner is stuck to the wall that says EFFIE FOR PRESIDENT in rainbow letters.

I feel a big lump appear in my throat as they all smile at me.

"We're really sorry, Effie," Dad says.

"We're always on your team," Mum chimes in. "We can't help worrying about you ... we *are* your parents, but if you want to do this, then we support you all the way."

I really think I might cry now and there's a little pause as I try and blink the pesky tears away.

"I was told there would be chocolate," Lil's voice breaks in loudly.

We all laugh then. Well, apart from Lil, who is folding her arms mutinously and muttering about Maltesers and how she won't be silenced with a "treat-sized" bag. Only full-sized confectionary is acceptable.

"Thank you," I choke out, while being bundled into a big group hug. "This is just SO what I needed today."

"Anything we can help with?" Mum asks.

"No," I say, "just something I need to do. Some stupid boys were going on about how girls can't play football and it made me cross."

Lil's eyes narrow dangerously. "What boys?" she asks. "Give me names. I can take care of it." She traces a line across her throat with her index finger. "I know people."

"How about instead of acting like a gangster, you lay the table, young lady." Mum rolls her eyes.

Lil huffs a loud sigh. "I'm so unappreciated."

"I appreciate you," I say. "I'll let you know if I need any legs breaking."

Lil gives me a thumbs up and disappears into the kitchen, whistling a happy tune.

"She *is* joking, isn't she?" Dad whispers, watching her retreating back.

"I think so," I reply. "But aren't you glad she's on *our* side?"

At the end of the week we have another campaign meeting. The cupboard is looking a lot better these days. Ruby and Jess are sprawled on the big purple cushions. The shelves are full of glitter pens and coloured card and blank sheets of paper. A VOTE FOR EFFIE banner is stuck along one wall. Kevin is sticking up another poster on the other wall.

"Oh, cool," Ruby says, going over to look. It turns out Kevin is really, REALLY good at art and he's covered the walls in brilliant drawings. This poster is a picture of me in a superhero outfit, my fist pumping in the air as I fly through the sky. On the ground below me are the rest of the team, cheering and waving and holding VOTE FOR EFFIE banners.

"I love it!" I exclaim.

Angelika looks at it, nodding. "We should photocopy this one and put it around the halls."

Kevin's ears turn pink. "I don't know if it's good enough for that. . ." he says.

"Don't be modest." Ruby slaps him on the arm. "It's wicked."

"It really looks like us," Jess says. "I'm even wearing my backpack." She points to the little drawing of herself with its funky black-and-pink bag.

Zo arrives then. She is still wearing her coat, but she has pulled her hood down, revealing her dark, shining hair pulled into two tight braids. She smiles tentatively as a chorus of "Hi, Zo!" and "All right, Zo?" fills the air. She slips in and takes up her position in the corner.

"OK," I say. "Now that we're all here, we need to start talking about the next phase for the campaign. The launch went pretty well. . ."

"Until we had to throw away my mum's biscuits," Kevin puts in.

"Yes," I agree, "that was a real shame."

"I could probably get her to make some for our meetings if you want?" he asks brightly.

There is a tense silence.

Jess opens her mouth but I cut her off very quickly.

"Er," I begin, "well, that's really kind, but I don't think we should be ... distracted by biscuits. No matter how ... delicious."

Kevin looks a bit shocked at this pronouncement, and I can't really blame him, because an anti-biscuit policy is not really my style at all, but the rest of the team look relieved and murmur in agreement.

"Important issues to focus on," Ruby mutters.

"Serious times," Angelika chimes in.

"Plus those biscuits were gross," Jess says.

"Anyway," I press on, "let's talk campaign details. I think it's time we started making a big splash, getting our campaign OUT THERE. Making sure everyone knows about all the amazing things we can do for the school. Getting our voices heard!"

Angelika nods, tapping a pencil against her cheek. She doesn't usually wear glasses, but she is sporting some now – although a closer look reveals that they are prop frames without any glass in them. She seems to be wearing them at the moment for the sole purpose of looking at us over the top of them. "With that in mind I've lined up an interview for Effie with the school newspaper to talk about the big campaign issues." The way she says it is like a real campaign manager. It's like she's got me a top spot on a chat show where the host will ask me earnest questions about my life and we'll both cry a bit about my incredible journey and then talk about recycling bins.

"Wow!" I exclaim. "How did you manage that?"

Angelika shrugs. "I have my contacts," she says mysteriously.

"Well, that will be a great start." I rub my hands together. "And if we plaster the school halls in posters that should help too."

"I think we need to find more ways to get your face out there, Effie," Ruby says. "No offence, but I think lots of people still don't actually know who you are."

"Only because you're new," Angelika adds quickly.

"That's a good point." I nod, scribbling furious notes into my campaign notebook. It is purple with pictures of General Organa and Rey from Star Wars and Hermione Granger carefully pasted all over it.

"You could do a drop-in session," Kevin suggests. "One lunchtime where people can come and talk to you about problems they're having. Then you can say how you would deal with them if you were president?"

"Kevin!" I exclaim. "That is such a good idea!"

"Nice one, Kev!" Ruby agrees. "People love having a good moan. It'll be really popular."

"It's perfect," I say, hugging my notebook to my chest. "It will give me a chance to meet people, and to let them know exactly what I'll be doing as president." I beam around the room at them all. "Brilliant work, team!"

CHAPTER *Eighteen*

The Highworth Grange Chronicle   Issue No. 203

WHO IS EFFIE KOSTAS?
CATRIONA MCGIDDENS MEETS THE SCHOOL'S NEWEST POLITICAL CANDIDATE

This week I sit down with Highworth Grange's answer to Hillary Clinton – new student Euphemia Kostas. Euphemia (who prefers to go by the name Effie) moved to Highworth Grange in October, but her short time at our school has been rocked by SCANDAL and DRAMA as she has decided to take on reigning junior class president, Aaron Davis, in our upcoming student council election.

As our readers well know, Aaron Davis was elected in a landslide victory last year – an unheard-of accomplishment for a year-eight student. Now, Aaron is ruling the junior school in year nine but he probably hadn't counted on the arrival of fresh-faced Effie Kostas as a potential rival for his throne.

WHO WILL SUCCEED IN THIS VICIOUS FIGHT FOR POWER?

I was initially contacted by Effie's campaign manager, Angelika Lisowski, and invited into the campaign's inner sanctum for an **EXCLUSIVE, NO HOLDS BARRED** interview. When asked why she supports the candidate, Angelika replied, "Effie Kostas is the **REAL DEAL**. She's so clever and funny, and her organizational skills are next level. You should see her Post-it note collection . . . there are shapes and colours I didn't even know existed."

I begin by asking Effie to share a little more information on her campaign with our readers. Her answer is really quite long and she talks very fast, but there's something about recycling in there, I think. But now that I've warmed her up, dear readers, it's time to get to the real nitty-gritty. To ask the hard-hitting questions that I know you want **ANSWERS** to.

WHY, I ask, did Effie decide to run for president?

Effie answers by quoting Beyoncé Knowles Carter: "Power is not given to you. You have to take it." Now as much as I **LOVE** Queen Bey, I think we all know that's not the **REAL ANSWER**. When I ask Effie if there was a particular **INCIDENT** that was really a turning point for her she immediately becomes **VERY SHIFTY**.

"Is this about Aaron Davis?" Effie asks.

Interesting that she should bring him up, dear readers. **VERY INTERESTING INDEED**. Is it true that a brawl over a slice of Victoria sponge was the dramatic scene of her decision to run?

Effie seems unnecessarily flustered by this question, but I can exclusively reveal that it was actually A PIECE OF **CHOCOLATE CAKE** at the centre of her dramatic eruption.

So, I ask, cutting to the heart of the matter with my excellent journalistic skills, is there anything between Effie and Aaron? Are they, perhaps, MORE than just political rivals?

Effie's face goes quite red and she starts mumbling something about a mentoring scheme but, like a **BLOODHOUND**, I know I have caught the scent of the true story. I've heard whispers from Aaron's camp that he thinks Effie has got a crush on him and that she's doing all of this to get his attention. I ask Effie what she has to say on the matter. "That's the most ridiculous..." she exclaims, angrily. "Honestly, I'd rather be boiled in oil than have anything to do with Aaron Davis. The idea that the **ONLY** reason I would run against him is because I fancy him is SO **INSULTING** that it makes me want to scream. Only **THEN** people would say I was being a hysterical GIRL and so I have to try and be **CALM AND COLLECTED**."

I don't know about you, but **METHINKS THE CANDIDATE DOTH PROTEST TOO MUCH**.

Does Effie have any final thoughts that she would like to share with the readers of the *Highworth Grange Chronicle*?

"Yes," she says, drawing herself up tall and staring nobly into the distance. "I would like all your readers to listen, really listen, to the candidates and to make their decision about who to vote for based on who makes the strongest arguments. I care about what you all want from the student council, and any ways in which you feel ignored or overlooked at the moment. I'm running a drop-in session at my campaign office next

Monday, 21 November, at lunchtime, and I invite you to come along and let me hear what **YOU** want from a student council president."

What **STIRRING** stuff, readers. I don't know about you, but I'm feeling inspired!

So, there you have it. **STRAIGHT FROM THE HORSE'S MOUTH**. It is, of course, the duty of this paper to remain impartial, but this reporter was certainly stirred by the **PASSION** and **ENTHUSIASM** shown by Ms. Kostas. As for whether there's anything more than rivalry between Effie and Aaron, that remains to be seen. So, are you **#TeamEffie** or **#TeamAaron**? Or, like us, are you secretly shipping **#EffRon**?

Let us know by sending us a snap **@HGChronicleRulez**.

CHAPTER *Nineteen*

"I just can't believe they gave us a cutesy couple name," I huff.

"You aren't *still* obsessing over that article, are you?" Angelika asks.

"And you have to admit that EffRon *is* a pretty good couple name," Jess pipes up. "Because your name is Effie and his name is Aaron." She chuckles.

"Zac Efron is SO buff," Ruby sighs dreamily.

"So buff," Kevin agrees.

"Zac Efron's buffness has nothing to do with it!" I cry, exasperated. "It's just... The very *idea* of it! That there's something going on with me and that ... that ... arrogant ... stuck-up ... MOON

HEAD!" I finish, borrowing from Lennon the parrot's impressive vocabulary.

"Do not speak dismissively of Zac Efron's bufficity," Ruby says solemnly. "No matter how angry you are."

"Sorry," I sigh. "I just wish that the interview had been about the campaign, instead of being about my rivalry with Aaron."

"It did say that you were full of passion and enthusiasm," Kevin points out, helpfully.

"And you did manage to mention your green initiative," Angelika adds reassuringly.

"I know, but we didn't even get to talk about raising money for the library, or the lunch buddy system so that no one has to eat their lunch alone." I deflate. "How will people get to hear all the good things we want to accomplish?"

"Well, that's what today is for, isn't it?" Angelika says sunnily. "You're going to meet loads of people and listen to them and talk about the ways you can improve their school lives."

"That's true." I brighten. The whole team is assembled at campaign HQ. The drop-in session is due to start in ten minutes. Aside from the newspaper article, we've put up lots of posters to advertise it, and Ruby has even been scaring the pants off people, thrusting leaflets into their hands and "suggesting" that they should turn up.

Ruby and Kevin are acting as bouncers on the door. As far as I can tell there's no reason for this. Turns out that Ruby wasn't actually joking when she recommended herself as head of security.

"You never know, boss," she says. "There could be someone who kicks off over the colour of the proposed recycling bins and then I have to swoop in and karate chop them." She sounds a bit too hopeful for my liking as she demonstrates a swift karate chop, slicing her hand through the air.

She and Kevin stand either side of the door with their hands folded in front of them, feet spread wide, stance menacing. Ruby is wearing a large pair of dark sunglasses.

"I think Kev and I should have walkie-talkies," she says for the third time. "As we're the security team."

"You're literally standing next to each other," Angelika points out. "What on earth would you do with the walkie-talkies?"

"Well, *obviously* we'd use them if we got split up chasing a perp," Ruby says, scornfully.

"I don't think there are going to be a lot of perps to chase down," I say soothingly.

"Don't you worry, Effie," Kevin says, pulling himself up to his full height and almost brushing my chin. "If anyone wants to get to you they have to get through us first. We won't let you down." He looks at me earnestly. "I'd take a bullet for you."

"Er – thanks," I manage.

"All part of the job." Kevin's voice is solemn. Ruby throws him an admiring glance. I have to say that Kevin has really been coming out of his shell over the last couple of weeks.

"*Anyway*," Angelika breaks in now, "we've got Ruby and Kevin on the door, making sure only one person gets in at a time. Jess and I are going to be talking to people in the queue to get an idea of their issue, which we will then write down on THESE colour-coordinated reference cards." Angelika fans out a pile of cards and waves them in the air. "A blue card is for academic problems, green for clubs and societies, pink for anything else. DOES EVERYONE UNDERSTAND THE SYSTEM?" Everyone nods obediently. I am full of admiration for my pal's organizational prowess. "REPEAT IT BACK TO ME," Angelika yells like a drill sergeant.

"Blue for academic, green for clubs and societies and pink for anything else," we all mutter.

"Excellent." Angelika nods approvingly. "Each visitor will get a maximum of five minutes with Effie. When they enter the room their reference card will be handed to Zo, who will give it to Effie." Zo nods here, and I feel a bit better that she's going to be in the room with me. While I greatly admire Angelika's efficiency, I have to admit it's making me a bit nervous. "Ruby will then start her stopwatch. At the four-minute point she will knock once as a warning to begin winding up the session. At five minutes she will knock three times and the visitor will leave, then the process begins again." Angelika casts an eagle eye over us. "Is everyone clear on their jobs? Are we all ready?"

"Yes!" we cry.

"Right." Angelika nods. "Then, places!"

Zo and I make our way in to the cupboard and I take my seat behind the table, leaving an empty chair across from me for my stream of visitors. As the silence inside the cupboard wraps itself around us, I can't stop the nervous feeling coiling inside my stomach.

"Um, Zo?" I say in a low voice.

Zo looks at me questioningly.

"I couldn't help but notice that there wasn't anyone

out there, queuing up to see me." The nervous feeling grows stronger. "What if no one comes?"

Zo stands awkwardly for a moment. I see her swallow. Then ... very slowly ... she reaches out one hand and pats my arm reassuringly.

"Thanks," I gulp. "I'm so glad you're here, by the way."

We share a smile, and then Ruby opens the door.

"First one is here!" she hisses, thrusting a pink card at Zo, who brings it over to me and then goes to stand in the corner.

I look down at the card. What does it say? Jess's writing is not the easiest to read. It looks a bit like "small UFOs". That can't be right ... can it? Although, I'll admit, a tiny alien invasion would be an interesting problem, presidentially speaking.

A girl appears in the doorway. She's from the year below, I think. Her reddish-brown hair is pulled up into a bouncy ponytail that bobs when she walks. She doesn't look like an alien, but I suppose you never know.

"Have a seat," I say with a smile, gesturing to the chair. "I'm Effie. How can I help you today?"

The girl sits down. "I already told that girl out there." She gestures back to the door.

"Yes, sorry," I say patiently, "I can't quite make out what she's written down here."

The girl huffs. "It's about school uniforms," she says.

"Ahhhhh." I lean back in my chair. "School uniforms. That makes more sense."

"More sense than what?" the girl asks, suspiciously.

"Nothing," I say quickly, "it doesn't matter. Sorry, what's your name?"

"Amy," the girl says.

"OK, Amy." I smile. "So you want to talk about school uniforms?"

"That's right." She nods. "I think we should have new ones. Better ones."

"Better?" I ask, puzzled. "What sort of improvements did you have in mind?"

"I don't know," Amy says thoughtfully. "I just think these black blazers are so frumpy. Maybe we could get a designer in to create new ones?"

"A designer?" I echo.

"Yes!" Amy is warming to her theme now. "You know, like Gucci or Stella McCartney. Could you sort that?"

"Could I get Gucci to redesign our school uniforms?" I say carefully, making sure I have understood what she's asking.

"Yeah." Amy nods eagerly. "Could you?"

"Um, well, no," I murmur. "I don't think so."

"Oh." Amy looks put out and folds her arms across her chest. "So you wouldn't even try?"

"Well, I wouldn't want to promise something I didn't think I could achieve," I say quickly, "but maybe we could talk to Ms Shaarawi about some smaller changes. I think the girls should definitely be allowed to wear trousers, for example, and I'd really like to get that changed."

"Hmm." Amy doesn't look too impressed.

There is a single knock on the door.

"So is there anything else you wanted to ask about?" I smile widely in what I hope is a friendly way.

"No." Amy gets to her feet. "Thanks anyway."

"You're welcome," I call after her. "I hope I can count on your vo—" I am cut short by the slamming of the door behind her.

After Amy is Gareth, who wants me to get pizza on the school menu every lunchtime, and then Sam, who thinks that we should only have school two days a week. Then there's Emily, who wants chips on the menu for lunch and thinks we should open a McDonald's franchise inside the school, and then Matt, who is another vote for pizza.

The door opens again and Ruby holds out another card, pink again. Zo collects it and brings it over to me. In Angelika's neat, round handwriting is written:

* *Alisha – year nine*
* *Wants to discuss school dinners.*

I sigh. "Hi, Alisha." I greet the girl who comes through the door with a smile. "Please, take a seat."

CHAPTER *Twenty*

The rest of the afternoon drags by pretty slowly. I try to concentrate on my geography lesson, but the room is so warm and the teacher's voice is so droning that I am fighting just to stay awake. I feel a bit deflated by the drop-in session. I had been hoping it would be a big opportunity for me to talk to people about the issues that matter to them. I suppose that what has surprised me the most in this whole campaigning business is that most people just don't seem that . . . *bothered* about things. Although I guess part of your job if you run for student council is to try and make people more aware of the issues that affect them.

I try to imagine how, years from now, in a documentary about my rise to power, my fellow students will be interviewed, tearfully talking about the way I changed their lives. "Effie just made us care," someone will say, through a broken sob. "Because of her we realized that things could change for the better if we just worked together." Then there will be stirring music and I will appear shaking my head modestly and enveloping them in a warm hug and then we'll both cry at how much we've grown and changed. I sigh happily, thinking about all the ways we can make a difference.

Take the girls' football team, for example. It has taken over a week of lunch breaks, but eventually me and Ruby have twelve whole names on our list. Fortunately, none of them is mine. If we couldn't find enough people then I would obviously have volunteered, but I'm pretty sure the team would not have benefitted from my participation. I have decided instead to be their biggest, most loyal fan. I am *really* good at waving banners and shouting.

It took a long time and a lot of people staring blankly at us like they couldn't work out what we were doing, but once word got around about the team, quite a few girls stopped by our sign-up table. Mostly they were just interested in what we were doing – and a few had obviously heard about my run-in with Aaron and wanted to know what all the fuss was about – but slowly, we started to get more names on the list. Even though not everyone signed up, there are lots of girls – like me – who aren't great at football but who really support the idea. I think that the team will have a big fan club at their first match. Ruby is definitely pleased, and she's roped her dad in to coach the team so Mrs Gregory has signed off on them using the field. AND all the equipment that was in our campaign HQ is finally going to be put to good use. Everyone wins.

Even though I am not school council president (not YET anyway) it is nice to feel like I can still make a difference. Even if it's just small things, a little bit at a time, it's good to see things change. There's going to be a girls' football team now and I enjoy thinking about Luke-the-baboon's face when they become a big success. That'll show him.

That evening Angelika comes over to our house for dinner and we don't talk about the campaign at all. Instead we do our maths homework up in my room as quickly as possible while munching on Lil's secret Haribo stash. As the sun sinks outside and we make our way downstairs, Dad lights a fire in the sitting room and a cosy glow falls over the rest of the night. It's actually really nice to have a break from the campaign and to remember that there is other important stuff going on, like takeaway pizza and cheesy action films and those sticky nose strip things that pull out all your blackheads and are so disgusting in the most satisfying way ever. We sit on the sofa with Lil, and Dad makes us strawberry milkshakes with real ice cream in and – after Lil makes a fuss – whipped cream on top as well. "AND THERE'D BETTER BE A FLAKE IN THERE TOO," Lil yells.

When Mum gets back from the library she does French plaits in our hair, which is the one skill that Dad can't seem to master, and as I sit on the floor with her fingers gently untangling my curls I feel really happy. When Angelika's mum arrives to pick her up we're in the middle of performing the Schuyler Sisters song from *Hamilton* and she comes inside to watch me, Angelika and Lil prance around, singing into our hairbrushes and thrusting our fists in the air.

Afterwards, Angelika leaves and I make my way upstairs, a contented sigh on my lips. It's nice to have such a good friend around.

"WHERE ARE ALL MY HARIBOOOOOOOO-OOOO????" Lil's voice shrieks then, disrupting my mellow mood quite dramatically.

Without another word I run the rest of the way upstairs. It's not that I'm scared of my little sister, I reason as I wedge a chair underneath my door handle ... not at all ... it's just that no sane person wants to be the one standing between her and her sugar fix.

CHAPTER *Twenty-One*

"So what we've learned is that people are really interested in school dinners," Angelika says brightly the next day. "That's useful campaign information."

"I suppose," I say glumly.

"So if we want to appeal to the other students we should have a campaign based on pizza and chips." Jess tips her head to the side, thoughtfully.

"But we're so much more than pizza and chips!" I exclaim.

"There's your next sandwich board," Ruby smirks.

Kevin barrels into the room. It's obvious he's been running. "Did you . . . see these?" he pants. His hands thrust forward, clutching a brightly coloured flyer.

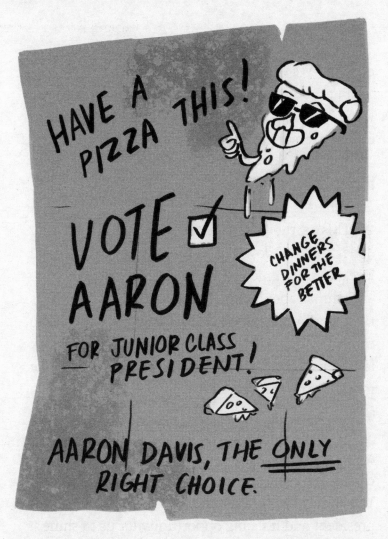

I stare at the leaflet with my mouth hanging open.

"I can't believe Aaron stole our campaign!" Jess says indignantly.

"Pizza was never our campaign," I say with great

dignity. "We've got real issues to talk about."

"But you have to give the voters what they want," Jess says, striking at the flyer in her hand to emphasize her point. "And they want pizza."

"You know what's more interesting about these leaflets," Angelika says.

"What?" I ask.

"This is the first campaigning Aaron's actually done at all." A slow smile spreads across Angelika's face. "I think it means you've got him rattled."

I think about this for a second. Angelika is right that Aaron has put absolutely zero effort into campaigning so far, while we've been hard at work for weeks. I feel a grin appearing on my face too. We must have him worried. My competitive spirit is wide awake now.

"Well, we'd better give him something to worry about then, hadn't we?" I say gleefully. "The next campaign event is the student fair on Monday. You have to have a stand to be in the running for president and it's a big opportunity for us to shine."

"I wonder if Aaron even knows you have to have a stand?" Angelika asks then. "After all, he seemed pretty in the dark about the debate until you told him about it."

"Oooh, that's a good point," I say. "Although it would be a bit rubbish beating him on a technicality."

The others look less convinced about this.

"OK, so with all the information we've learned at the drop-in session, what theme do you think we should have?" I ask after a brief pause, returning to the matter of the fair. "It has to be something that represents our campaign." I look over at Kevin, our resident artist. "Have you got any ideas?"

"Well, actually," Ruby grins, nudging Kevin with her elbow. "Me and Kev have been talking about it. I was reading about this woman called Mary Read from, like, the seventeenth century who dressed up as a man and became a soldier and then later she became this wicked pirate woman who ruled the seven seas with her best mate Anne Bonny, and they were totally ferocious and brilliant. We thought maybe we could do a pirate theme for the stand and talk a bit about how they were these cool women in a men's world who refused to just sit at home and be quiet. They made their voices heard. Just like you, Effie."

I can't help but grin at that.

Kevin reaches into his backpack. "I did some rough sketches. We thought we could make the stand look like a ship. And then pirate costumes are really easy for everyone?" He holds out the drawings that he has done.

"Wow!" I exclaim. "These are amazing! Are you guys sure you don't mind doing all that work?"

Ruby and Kevin shake their heads. "It won't actually be that much work," Ruby says confidently. "We just paint the sides of the boat on to some big pieces of cardboard, and then we make a sail out of a sheet."

"I've got some blue cloth we can use for the water," Angelika says, peering over my shoulder at the drawings.

"And I can make the biscuits!" Kevin volunteers cheerfully.

"NO!" we all cry in one voice.

"I'll make the biscuits," I say quickly. "I can get Lil to help me. And you've all done so much for me." I smile mistily. "You guys are the best campaign team a girl could ask for."

Lil and I end up going to Iris's house to make the biscuits at the weekend. Lil mentioned them at one of their Disney marathons and Iris invited us. Apparently she has the best gingerbread recipe in town.

With the biscuits cooling on the side, filling the

air with their spicy, gingery smell, we assemble our piping bags and the different coloured icing and the edible glitter. These are going to be the most spectacular pirate biscuits anyone has ever seen.

"I'm going to make a hot pink skull and crossbones with purple glitter and rainbow sprinkles," Lil says thoughtfully.

"Nice," I say. "What are you going to do first, Iris?" I ask.

Iris is eyeing the decorations with a look of distaste. "I don't know," she grunts, but her fingers close around the gold glitter, and I can see a gleam in her eyes.

"PUNY HUMAN!" Lennon croaks.

Lil giggles. "I taught him that one," she says proudly. "I'm trying to get him to sing with me. Hey, Lennon," she coos, "DO YOU WANNA BUILD A SNOWMAAAAAN?"

"NOT ON YOUR LIFE, SUNSHINE!" Lennon grumbles.

"And I taught him that one!" Iris cackles.

We work quietly for a minute, spangling our biscuits and generally making a bit of a mess.

"So, how is the campaign going?" Iris asks.

"It's OK," I sigh. "It's hard work. It just feels like

people aren't really interested."

Iris nods knowingly. "That's always the way," she agrees. "Getting people to change their attitude is the hard bit."

"I think if we do a good job on our stand at the fair then that could make a bit of a splash." I shake the rainbow sprinkles on to the biscuit in front of me with great enthusiasm. "Get people to pay attention. I feel like if I could just get them to listen, to really hear what I'm saying. . ." I trail off.

"Well, you just have to make your stand spectacular then," Iris says firmly. "It's no good being shy and retiring. You take up some space, Effie. You've got a big voice. Don't be afraid to use it."

"NOISY PEANUT!" Lennon whistles.

"That's right, Lennon," Iris says. "She needs to be a very noisy peanut."

I look thoughtfully at Lennon. I think I am having a major brainwave as to how we can make our stand be the one that people remember.

"Actually, Iris. . ." I say. "I wonder if I can ask you for a huge favour?"

CHAPTER *Twenty-Two*

The fair is set to take place on Monday after school. My team have been hard at work over the weekend and I am hoping that all of that hard work is about to pay off.

We gather in the school hall, where rows of tables have been placed around the edge of the room. The tables have bits of paper stuck to the front with tape and we find the one with my name on it.

"Prime location," Angelika says in a satisfied tone, and the others murmur in agreement. I, on the other hand, have noticed something that is less than ideal about the placement of our stand.

"Oh no," I mutter, eyeing the sign on the table next to ours.

"What's up, Kostas?" Aaron Davis saunters up beside me. "Looks like we're neighbours."

"So I guess you worked out you needed to be here in the end?" I grind out.

"I don't know why you sound so surprised." Aaron raises an eyebrow here. "I can do my homework too. I *am* student council president."

"For now," I mutter, defiantly.

"And so I *do* attend these sorts of events anyway," Aaron continues airily, ignoring me completely. "You're not the only person who cares about the school, you know," he adds, and there's something defiant in his tone.

"You could have fooled me," I snort.

"Look," Aaron says, keeping his voice annoyingly calm. "I don't get what you're so upset about. Everything was running fine before you came in and started making a big, giant fuss and messing around with things. There's really no need for you to be so ... so. . ."

"So *what*?" I ask dangerously. "Just because I think you could do more with the influence you have," I say, "doesn't mean I'm 'messing around' with things. Anyway," I sniff, "I think we should be having a civil campaign, keeping things nice and polite. I'm not doing anything wrong."

"Is that what you call it when you say you want to boil someone in oil in the school paper?" Aaron tips his head to one side as though considering this.

"Well, at least I didn't tell a reporter that you were ONLY running against me because you FANCY me," I flash back, stung. I can feel my cheeks starting to burn, but I keep my most impressive glower on my face.

Aaron's cheeks actually go a bit pink then as well. "I don't know who said that to Cat," he mumbles, "but it definitely wasn't me."

I shrug elaborately, as if I couldn't care less. "It doesn't matter anyway," I say, and my voice is coming out all sharp and flinty. "Because it is definitely NOT TRUE. Not a bit. Not in a million years. Never. Never. NEVER. I would NEVER fancy you."

"Yeah, well, believe me, the feeling is mutual," Aaron snaps. "I like nice girls."

"Nice girls? Nice girls?! What does that even mean? 'NICE GIRLS' IS A THING BOYS SAY AND THE WHOLE IDEA IS INVENTED TO MAKE SURE WE STAY QUIET AND SMALL AND POLITE!" I yell. Aaron is looking at me wide-eyed and I take a deep breath. "I am a very nice girl, thank you," I say then coldly, getting my voice under control. "But I don't want to be pushed around, and I am not going to be quiet."

"Yeah, that bit is actually fairly obvious," Aaron says, sticking a finger in his ear and wincing.

I glare at him, and he glares back.

"I'd better get back to my stand," I say. "My whole team have worked really hard on it." I look around. "Where are your team?" I ask.

"I don't have a *team*," Aaron snorts, "I'm not running for prime minister. This is hardly a real election, is it?"

"It's a shame that *you* don't care more about your own campaign because you are going to kick yourself when you lose," I say sweetly.

"I don't lose," Aaron says, and there's something steely in his words.

"This time you will," I taunt him.

"I don't think so," Aaron replies, and he's being so patronizing I want to scream. "Look, I suppose I underestimated you at the beginning... I didn't think you'd really go through with it, and that you would take it SO seriously. I actually think it's kinda *sweet*." He crinkles his nose here and I feel like I might be about to start breathing fire. In fact, I have a lovely daydream about turning into a dragon and incinerating him so that all that remains is a small pile of dust and a pair of football boots. And on his grave it would say, HERE LIES AARON DAVIS. HE TOLD A GIRL SHE WAS "KINDA SWEET" BUT SHE TURNED OUT TO BE A FIRE-BREATHING DRAGON. #AWKWARD

"Why are you smiling like that?" Aaron asks, breaking into my lovely imaginary funeral arrangements. He looks a bit startled by the obvious joy in my expression.

"No reason," I say. "Please. Carry on telling me how *sweet* I am."

"Oh, well," Aaron shuffles. "Not *you*, but the way you're so into it all. But I don't think you realize how things work here yet. I wouldn't want you to be humiliated..."

"The only person who is going to be humiliated is YOU," I crack back. This is DANGEROUSLY close to what Matt said, and the rattled, nervous feeling that conversation gave me makes an unwelcome reappearance. Is this a conspiracy between them? I can just see the two of them together deciding to try to intimidate me out of running.

"If you really think that, then you're delusional." Aaron's voice is getting louder now.

"YOU ARE!" I hiss.

"NO, YOU ARE!" Aaron snaps, and it's like we're both five years old but I can't help it, he makes me so cross. This is also the first time I've actually seen Aaron get annoyed, and I feel a strange sense of victory that I have at least shaken him out of his bored shrugging.

"HA!" I crow. "WHAT A COMEBACK."

Aaron glowers and opens his mouth to reply before stopping short. I swing around then to find Miss Sardana standing behind me. From the look on her face it's clear that she heard quite a lot of our argument. I guess we weren't exactly being quiet.

"Is there a problem here?" she asks, and though her tone is mild, her eyes are very alert.

"No, miss," we both mumble.

"I should hope not," Miss Sardana says. "I would expect far better behaviour from members or potential members of our student council." Her eyes bore into mine here, and I feel a wave of shame wash over me.

"Sorry," I say.

"Yeah, sorry," Aaron echoes.

Miss Sardana gives us one beadier stare that says very clearly "I have my eye on you" before walking off to organize people.

I give Aaron a cold smile and turn back to my team, who are all hovering nearby, mouths agape, clearly listening very carefully to the exchange.

"Why are you all standing around?" I grumble, a blush spreading across my face. "We've got lots to get on with."

"Aye aye, Captain," Ruby salutes. "And by the way," she whispers, "*that* was awesome!"

CHAPTER Twenty-Three

It takes me a while to get my breathing back to normal and my temper under control. I notice my hands are shaking as I start unpacking our bags. By the time our stand is assembled I have almost calmed down, and I must admit that the team have outdone themselves. The table has become the front of a pirate ship, two large sheets of cardboard propped in a V shape at its sides. These have been painted by Kevin and Ruby to look like the sides of the boat. Angelika has swirled blue silky material around the floor at the front and there are seashells and rubber ducks scattered across it. Behind the table, on a broom attached to a chair, a sheet has been stretched out like a sail, and there's even a Jolly Roger flag hanging from the top. Kevin has made a sign that features a drawing of me dressed as a pirate captain and it says, EFFIE KOSTAS: STEERING HIGHWORTH GRANGE IN THE RIGHT DIRECTION.

The whole thing looks almost as impressive as we do with everyone in costume. I think Kevin's outfit might be the best; his enormous black hat capped with a curling white feather, and a bushy stick-on beard gives him a very salty sea dog vibe. Ruby and Jess are brandishing cutlasses in a rather menacing fashion. Ruby's crimson-and-black-striped trousers are very dramatic, especially coupled with a silky black shirt, and I don't know how she's doing it, but she makes blacked-out teeth and an eyepatch look

good. Angelika's pirated up her Alexander Hamilton costume, and she seems to have tracked down her duelling pistol again. My own costume is a sort of feisty pirate princess look with big gold hoop earrings and a red scarf wrapped around my hair. Even Zo has a stuffed parrot perched on the shoulder of her usual Puffa jacket. We carefully lay out the colourful, sparkly biscuits on trays on the table and strike our poses behind them. The whole effect is pretty spectacular.

"Anne and Mary would be proud," Angelika says.

"Anne and Mary would probably tie us all up and steal our biscuits," I point out.

"So cool," Ruby murmurs with shining eyes.

Aaron has been watching the whole thing and looking increasingly grumpy. His stand seems to consist of a bit of paper bunting covered in footballs and a plastic tub full of chocolate brownies that he has obviously bought from a shop. I'm surprised he hasn't brought a pizza with him. I resist the urge to point out that he's not even making the most of his own rubbish policies.

"I see you've made the absolute BARE MINIMUM effort," I hiss as I arrange some green streamers to look like seaweed. "Is that what your stand says about your campaign? Seems about right."

Aaron just rolls his eyes in response and slumps into the chair behind his table.

I'm so excited, waiting for the arrival of the parents, because I know that Dad is bringing the finishing touch for our stand, and our secret weapon. When the doors finally open, he is one of the first through them, because I have him very well trained and I drilled him five times this morning on the fastest route to the school. I also told him it started fifteen minutes earlier than it really did, just to make double sure he would be on time. From the look of his and Lil's pink noses and grumpy expressions, that was an unnecessary step. What can I say though, it's always best to be prepared.

In one of Dad's hands is a large dome-shaped object, covered in a pale blue sheet. From the way Dad is walking you can tell it's quite heavy.

He sets the object down on the extra table we have set up at the back of our stand.

"Thanks, Dad," I beam, whipping the sheet away to reveal Lennon the parrot perched in a nifty little travelling cage.

"You have got to be kidding me," I hear Aaron mutter.

"GIBBERING IDIOT!" Lennon squawks at him.

"Such a gooooood booooy," I croon, offering him a nut from my pocket and throwing a smirk at Aaron.

The others have all crowded around.

"Wow! A real parrot!" Kevin says.

"WHAT A LOSER," Lennon responds.

Iris didn't mind a bit about us borrowing Lennon. She said it was nice for him to have a change of scenery. Miss Sardana was harder to persuade. At first I wanted to have Lennon perched on my shoulder like a real pirate, but she said absolutely not. Finally, she agreed we could bring him as long as he stayed in his cage, well away from the food. I knew he was going to be the star attraction of the fair and the perfect way to lure people over to our stand, especially as Lil volunteered to stand beside the cage and bribe him with treats to bow and whistle to people.

"Have a biscuit, Dad," I say, choosing him one of the best-looking ones.

"Oh, thanks," he says, taking it off me.

"That'll be 50p, please," I sing, sweetly.

"What, even after all my hard work?" Dad asks.

"We're raising money for the school." I roll my eyes. "If you really want to deprive innocent children of a better education then I suppose you can have it for free. . ."

"Stop! Wouldn't want that," Dad says, fumbling in his pocket and pulling out some change. "I'll take two, please – one for Lil as well."

"I want a purple one," Lil calls from where she is perched on a stool beside Lennon.

More people are starting to trickle through the doors, and just as I had hoped, our brilliant stand is attracting a big crowd. Lots of our fellow students and their parents want to come and see Lennon, but they also stop to tell Ruby and Kevin what a great job they've done on the decorations, or to compliment our costumes. I am feeling increasingly smug – especially as Aaron's stand is being totally ignored and his face is getting more and more sulky.

Ruby and I are handing out biscuits as fast as we can, and our little pot is filling up with coins.

"Top biscuits, Effie," a girl calls to me. Her name is Sophia, and she's in the year above. I feel a little glow that she knows who I am. A few weeks ago I was anonymous, a stranger – no one knew me and I felt like I hardly existed.

"Thanks!" I exclaim. "My sister helped to make them." Lil waves jauntily from her seat and Sophia waves back.

"Effie's good at loads of things, Soph." Ruby leans over now. "Don't forget she's running for student council president."

"Yeah, I know," Sophia says. "I saw your posters. Pretty cool artwork. And you're the one who helped start the girls' football team, right? You've got my vote."

It's like the world goes into slow motion as the words come out of Sophia's mouth. "Yooooou've goooooooooooot myyyyyyyyyy vooooooooooote."

A VOTE! Someone is going to vote for me, because of the things I've done. It's magic, it feels like winning, like I've been electrified and my skin is buzzing and crackling with untold energy. Maybe I'm a superhero now. Maybe I can actually make things happen with my mind. I feel unstoppable.

"Thanks," I beam, striking a superhero pose with my hands on my hips. "That's brilliant." As I turn around I catch Aaron's eye. He's obviously overheard, and he looks as if he's just sucked on a lemon. I feel my grin stretch even wider, even though I obviously can't make things happen with my mind ... being as he's STILL THERE.

The time passes quickly now, and before long

we're down to our last few biscuits. I notice that Aaron's friends have finally turned up. Katie is perched on the table beside the box of brownies, her legs swinging back and forth. She's applying a fresh coat of bubblegum-pink gloss to her lips in a hand mirror. Aaron's friend Luke is sprawled in the seat beside him, and the two of them are comparing text messages on their phones. Matt is here as well, although he's drifting around the room looking at all the different stands. I can see the top of his golden head winding through the crowds.

A cluster of boys turn up and they all exchange elaborate handshakes and one or two of them fish out some coins to buy a brownie.

"I don't know why you even bother with all this stuff," one of the boys says. "Why don't you finish early and come back to Beanie's with us?"

I fiddle with the trays in front of me, careful not to give away the fact that I am listening in to this.

"Nah," Aaron says. "I have to be here. Part of the student president thing."

"This student president thing is rubbish," Luke grumbles. "It's not even like you get anything out of it apart from the lunch pass."

"Yeah, well, you seem to like that a lot when I use

it to get your lunch too," Aaron says, "Anyway, it's good for my record. Especially if I'm senior president too, you know that. It'll help with getting into a good sixth form."

I'm surprised by this. Aaron Davis doesn't seem like the sort of boy who gives much thought to the future. It's hard to imagine him having ambition.

"You're such a dork," Luke scoffs, but it's quite friendly.

"I like it," Katie puts in. "You will too, when he's your gazillionaire boss one day."

Aaron grins at her and she smiles back, flipping her hair over her shoulder. Luke laughs noisily and the other boys join in.

Aaron looks over at me then, and the grin is still lingering on his face. Our eyes meet and my heart bangs in my chest with a loud, hollow thump.

"WHAT A DISASTER," Lennon intones gloomily as everyone around him claps.

CHAPTER *Twenty-Four*

The next day I feel like I'm floating around school. The fair was such a big success for us. We raised almost forty pounds and people seemed genuinely interested in what we had to say, even listening to me talk about our different campaign issues. This could be partly because Ruby insisted on a grizzly re-enactment of Mary Read and Anne Bonny's piratical adventures using a lot of ketchup as fake blood. Lil was enraptured, of course, and she has a new heroine ... although whether it's Mary Read or Ruby is not quite clear.

I'm still cross about my argument with Aaron. Just because he's reasonably good-looking and has a nice smile doesn't mean I'm about to forget all the insults he has piled upon my head. "*Sweet*", indeed. SWEET LIKE A TOOTHACHE. Ooh, that's good, I think. Why couldn't I have had such a witty comeback at the time of the argument? Now I feel annoyed with Aaron all over again.

Still, *victory* is certainly sweet, and even the tiniest taste of it like I had last night is putting me in the very best of spirits. My good mood lasts all the way through my double maths lesson where I have no problem in finding X at all... "Must be my new-found pirate skills," I say to Angelika, who snorts with laughter. Even when the teacher comes over to tell us to stop being noisy, we can hardly smother our giggles.

In fact, my good mood lasts almost all day, until 2.30 to be precise, when, on my way to my last lesson of the day, I run into Aaron. Quite literally.

"Why can't you look where you're going?" I snap from the floor where I have tumbled in a not very elegant heap.

Aaron holds his hand out to help me up, but I ignore it, angrily scrambling to my feet and pushing my wild curls out of my eyes.

"Why don't *you* look where *you're* going?" he snaps back, stuffing his hands into his pockets. It seems I'm not the only one who's been thinking about our fight. We glower at each other, a silence building between us that starts to feel suffocating.

"SWEET LIKE A TOOTHACHE!" I yell, finally, the words bursting from me before I can give them much thought. And actually, now that I've said it out loud, I'm not totally sure this comeback even makes sense.

Aaron looks completely confused, and I guess I can't blame him, but it doesn't stop me from feeling mad at him. I can hear all his patronizing words yesterday, piling on top of Matt's words and ringing in my ears. "Because of what you said last night," I say hotly. "About me being sweet."

Aaron huffs out a big sigh. "I cannot believe you are *still* droning on about that," he groans. "I'm sorry I said you were *acting* kinda sweet. I didn't realize it was the worst insult in the world. Why are you making such a big drama out of things?"

"I guess we can't all be as cool and laid-back as you," I snap. "Mostly because then nothing would EVER GET DONE."

"That is *enough*," a sharp voice comes from behind me. I shut my eyes for a second before turning to see Miss Sardana standing there, again, looking at me with weary disappointment, *again*. "I have already warned the pair of you about this unacceptable behaviour. Here at Highworth Grange we do not *brawl* in the corridors. You two will be at the student council meeting after school where we will discuss a fitting punishment. In the meantime I do not want to see any more of this silly fighting. Is that understood?"

"Yes, miss," I mumble, looking at my shoes.

"Yes, miss," I hear Aaron murmur as well.

"Right," Miss Sardana says. "Now, get on to your lessons."

Highworth Grange School Council Meeting – Tuesday 29 November

Minutes recorded by Angelika Lisowski

Meeting called to order at 3.30 p.m. by meeting chair Miss Sardana.

Members present:

Chair Miss Sardana
Aaron Davis (junior student president)

Matt Spader (junior student vice president)

Angelika Lisowski (junior student secretary)

Luna Stanworth (junior student treasurer)

Effie Kostas (top presidential candidate)

Reading of Agenda

Miss Sardana explains that she has invited Effie Kostas to the meeting because she is worried about the increasing hostility between her and Aaron Davis in their bid for student council president. Even though this is obviously, objectively, Aaron's fault.

New Business

- Miss Sardana explains that she has come up with a plan to get Effie and Aaron to work together. She is putting them in charge of the Winter Dance taking part on 9 December. This is typically handled by the student council treasurer, but as Luna is away at a netball tournament, Miss Sardana sees this as a way of "killing two birds with one stone".

- Effie Kostas has leapt to her feet. She is

angry that she has to work with Aaron and also strongly feels that a dance of this scale cannot be thrown together in under two weeks. (She is not wrong either. Goodness, think of the to-do list, although if anyone can pull this off, it's Effie Kostas, who is running for student president. VOTE FOR EFFIE!)

- Effie is rocking on her feet now and saying things like "FOOD" and "BAND" but also I think she just yelped the words "CONFETTI CANNON" in a very panicked tone.
- Aaron remains seated. He looks bored and a bit annoyed. Matt whispers something in his ear and they both laugh.
- Effie is shouting at them now, burning with the righteous anger of a thousand suns.
- Luna Stanworth reminds everyone that she has to get to netball practice.
- Miss Sardana has interrupted and pointed out that this is exactly the problem she is talking about. She's had enough of their behaviour.
- Effie has whipped out a notebook and pen. She is asking many questions; Miss Sardana is struggling to keep up. Effie's voice is

getting higher and higher, and her pen is flying across the page at such a speed that it might have someone's eye out in a minute. It's quite a nice pen actually, must ask her where she got that. The ink is purple with just the right amount of sparkle.

- Luna Stanworth just wants to note that she has to get to netball practice soon.

- Effie replies that netball practice is the least of anyone's worries, and that this is a level five emergency situation and that she doesn't understand why everyone is so calm.

- Angelika Lisowski agrees with her. And not just because best friends should always have each other's backs, but because – as a totally impartial observer – Effie is completely right and Aaron is totally wrong.

- Aaron suggests they can "just throw something together" and I swear Effie's hand twitches. Is she going to throw her pen at him?

- Matt agrees with Aaron that Effie should stop "making such a fuss". QUELLE SURPRISE.

- Aaron has asked Miss Sardana a sensible

question about the budget. He has pulled out his OWN notebook. Effie looks like she's about to fall off her chair.

- Miss Sardana says that Aaron and Effie have to make plans to meet up and finish the discussion. The dance is important and she wants to know they will do a good job.
- With a very big sigh, Aaron suggests his house.
- Effie describes this as ENEMY TERRITORY and says she will NEVER darken his doorstep and that the meeting should be at HER house.
- Aaron says fine and "who cares".
- Effie slumps in her chair. Even though she has won that argument, I think she has just realized that she has invited her mortal enemy and political nemesis over for tea. This could be bad. Really bad.
- Luna Stanworth leaves for netball practice

Meeting adjourned at 4.00 p.m.

CHAPTER *Twenty-Five*

This is my nightmare. I cannot BELIEVE that I have to work with Aaron Davis. I cannot BELIEVE that I have to be in charge of planning something as important as a school dance with him. And I also cannot BELIEVE we have less than two weeks to do it. What was Miss Sardana thinking? This kind of outrageous lack of organization will not stand when I am school council president, let me tell you that right now.

Also in the list of things I can't believe is that I am currently flitting nervously around my house, tidying up and waiting for Aaron Davis to turn up. At my house. My. House. Talk about weird.

"Get rid of this!" I hiss to my dad, snatching up a

photo of two-year-old me, smiling and gappy-toothed in the bath.

Dad looks a little alarmed at the manic light that I'm sure is burning in my eyes.

"Why are you getting so loopy?" Lil asks. Much to my despair, she has gone full Olaf. From her position slumped on the floor she looks like a melted marshmallow.

"Do you think you might like to get changed?" I ask Lil as sweetly as possible, but even I can hear the slight note of hysteria in my voice.

Lil tips her giant, carrot-adorned head to one side. "No," she says, equally sweetly. "I don't think so."

"I think you need to calm down a bit, Effie," Dad says in his most soothing voice. It sounds like he's talking to a nervous horse who is about to bolt. "Everything is going to be fine."

"You don't know that," I say in tragic tones. "This whole thing is a disaster. My mortal enemy, my arch-nemesis, is about to descend on us, and it's like you two don't even care!"

"I just don't get it," Lil says. "Tell us again why this boy is your mortal enemy?"

"I told you," I say weakly, "he stole my chocolate cake, he told me I would lose, he refused to take me or the campaign seriously … he called me *sweet*." This last bit is a growl as I tick things off on my fingers.

"To be honest, Effie," Lil says, "none of that sounds that bad."

"You had to be there," I grumble.

"It's nothing compared to my rivalry with George Petikis." Lil's face darkens.

"Why?" I ask, intrigued. "What did George Petikis do?"

Lil cracks her knuckles, threateningly. "Oh, he knows what he did," she says mysteriously. I decide it's best to let that one go.

Just then the doorbell rings.

"Gaaaaah!" I exclaim. Lil and Dad eye me with pity. I pull my shoulders back and go to answer the door.

Standing on the doorstep, I find that I am almost as tall as Aaron. His dark, shiny hair is all tousled and he's wearing a big coat and a yellow woolly scarf.

"Hi," he says flatly, and he has the look of someone who is about to be led to the guillotine.

"Hi," I reply. "I suppose you'd better come in." I step grudgingly aside.

Aaron follows me in, dragging his feet across the floor. In the sitting room, Lil has jumped up.

"Hello," she says, eyeing him narrowly.

"Hi," Aaron replies in quite a friendly way actually. "Nice Olaf costume."

"Thanks." Lil straightens one of the sleeves. "My dad made it."

"Cool," Aaron replies. I look at him, bewildered. "I have a little sister, too," he says, shrugging.

"Does she make you sing duets with her as well?" I ask unthinkingly.

Aaron smiles, and his nose crinkles up a bit. "Yeah," he laughs. "I always have to be Hans."

Lil looks at him with obvious glee. "I'll go and get my CD!" she cries. "Dad's hidden it in the laundry basket." She rolls her eyes. "So predictable."

"No thanks, Lil," I say quickly as Aaron's eyes widen in alarm. "We've got work to do."

Lil's bottom lip sticks out. "Oh," she pouts.

"Maybe some other time," Aaron says.

"OK," Lil smiles, and I swear she bats her eyelashes. For goodness' sake – is everyone that easily won over by Aaron?

At that moment Dad comes in. "Hi!" he exclaims. "You must be Aaron. I'm Dimitri."

"Hello." Aaron smiles politely.

"Do you guys want to grab some drinks and snacks from the kitchen?" Dad asks. "I understand that brain food is needed today."

We follow Dad into the kitchen, where I make two big glasses of squash and Dad and Aaron argue over whether Hobnobs or custard creams are the superior biscuit choice. I glower at them. It seems Aaron is working some kind of charm spell on all of my family.

"Right, well, I guess we should go upstairs then," I say with all the enthusiasm of a lump of ice. "This dance isn't going to plan itself."

Aaron obediently grabs the plate of biscuits and we go up to my room. Aaron goes straight over to my bookcases and starts having a good nosy around.

"You've got a lot of books," he says.

"I like to read," I say, awkwardly. I sort of hover in the middle of the room, unsure where I should sit or what I should do.

"Hmm." Aaron makes a non-committal sort of noise. He doesn't look awkward or uncomfortable at all. I wonder what he is thinking. What *I'm* thinking is that it's quite personal looking at someone's bookshelves. All of my favourite books say so much about me, it's like seeing into someone's soul. I watch his eyes move past my well-loved Roald Dahl collection, the tattered Malory Towers books that I read, dreaming of being shipped off to boarding school. He pauses on the three different complete sets of the Harry Potter books.

"Oh, wow!" he exclaims suddenly, pulling a book off the shelf. "*My Neighbor Totoro*! I love the film. I didn't know there was a book as well."

"Oh yeah, it's great." I am immediately caught up in his enthusiasm. "You can borrow it if you like." The words are out of my mouth before I can stop them.

Aaron looks at me in surprise. "Really?" A little frown puckers his forehead. "That would be great, thanks." He looks down at the book in his hands.

An awkward silence fills the air.

I clear my throat nervously and perch on the edge of my bed, gesturing to the desk chair across from me. "Why don't you sit down so we can get on with planning this thing?" I say, and it comes out a bit sharp and pointy.

"Sure." Aaron shrugs and flops into the chair. He opens his backpack and pulls out a notebook.

I reach under the bed and pull out the shiny new

ring binder that I have dedicated to this project. It is already full of bits of paper separated by colour-coded dividers.

"Wow," Aaron says, and he looks a bit dazed.

"I've already done a lot of research," I say, "using the details Miss Sardana gave us."

"Yeah." Aaron nods. "I can see that." He reaches out and takes the folder, flipping it open. "Category: decorations," he reads. "Subcategory: balloons; sub-subcategory: balloons, novelty shapes; sub-sub-subcategory: balloons, novelty shapes, animals." His eyes widen. "Wow, this is . . . intense."

"Yes, well." I snatch the folder back from him before he can realize there are a further eight subcategories in this section. "I like to be thorough." I tap my fingers on the front of the folder. "Anyway, I think the main thing we need to decide is what theme we're going with, then it's pretty easy. Miss Sardana has already organized the food and drink so our main responsibility is the decorations."

"Sure," Aaron says, flipping open his notebook. "Well, I had a couple of ideas."

I'm so surprised that he's done any preparation that I just stare at him. It must be pretty easy to read my expression because he quirks an eyebrow.

"There's no need to look like that," he says. "I *have* organized things before. In case you haven't noticed, I've been doing this job for almost a year now."

"I suppose I just didn't think you took it that seriously," I say.

Aaron snorts. "You mean I don't take it as seriously as you do."

I think about this. "Well . . . yes," I say finally. "But it's not a bad thing to take it seriously."

"I guess," Aaron sighs. "Why do you care so much? Isn't it exhausting caring about every little thing?"

"I've never really thought about it." I shrug. "I just see the thing that needs doing, and I want to do it the best I can."

Aaron is quiet, his face thoughtful. "And you don't think I've been doing my best?" he asks.

"Maybe you haven't been doing a *bad* job, exactly," I admit grudgingly. "But think how much better it could be. I want to use my voice to champion for others, to make sure that they're heard and listened to."

There's a pause.

"Well, I guess I'm going to have to start campaigning for real now," Aaron says. "I hope you're ready for some serious competition."

I raise an eyebrow at him. "Bring it on," I say.

CHAPTER *Twenty-Six*

SHOCK POLL REVEALS THE FIGHT FOR STUDENT COUNCIL PRESIDENT IS NECK AND NECK!

By Catriona McGiddens

An official poll of students reveals a tight race between current junior class president Aaron Davis and newcomer Effie Kostas.

In a recent survey undertaken in the canteen at lunchtime, this newspaper discovered **SHOCKING** results, revealed **EXCLUSIVELY** here.

When asked, over 40% of students* revealed they would be voting for new student and underdog candidate Effie Kostas. This result should upset those on TeamAaron, who assumed his victory was a certainty.

When asked about her choice, an Effie Kostas voter (who wishes to remain anonymous) said that she was swayed by Effie's **ENTHUSIASM** and passion. "She obviously cares about the school," our source said. "And she really listens to people. I never really thought the student council could do much before, but she wants to make a lot of changes. I think that's **INSPIRING**."

Aaron Davis supporter Ed says that Aaron is the **"OBVIOUS CHOICE"**. When asked why he thought this, Ed was unfortunately called away to watch a YouTube video of a dog on a skateboard and didn't respond.

Up to this point Aaron Davis has been considered a definite winner for the job, relying mostly on his reputation to clinch support while Effie has been hitting the streets. But with only thirteen days to the election, can Effie claw herself an unexpected victory, or will the tide remain in Aaron's favour? I guess only **TIME** will **TELL**.

Meanwhile, this reporter has heard that Aaron Davis was spotted entering Effie Kostas's house last night. Sources **INSIDE THE ADMINISTRATION** reveal that the two candidates have to plan the Winter Dance together. **"SPARKS WERE DEFINITELY FLYING,"** my source (who wishes to remain anonymous for legal reasons) confirmed before leaving for netball practice. Whether these two are rivals or something more remains a mystery, but one thing is for sure ... all eyes will be on them at the dance next week.

* This poll was based on a sample of the school population. This dedicated reporter talked to over twelve students to obtain these figures. Note: this may or may not be an accurate representation of the way the voting works out.

CHAPTER *Twenty-Seven*

In the end, Aaron and I settle on a "Winter Wonderland" theme. It might seem a bit predictable, but at such short notice I know we need a straightforward theme if we are going to pull off my spectacular vision.

Much to my surprise, the planning process is actually going OK. After that first conversation in my room Aaron and I don't discuss the campaign again, although I notice that lots of VOTE FOR AARON posters begin appearing alongside the Effie posters in the hallways, and I have seen quite a few people wandering around with #TeamAaron badges on. (I am pretty mad with myself for not thinking of doing badges, actually.) It really does seem as though Aaron is finally taking the campaign seriously, and it's quite a relief to feel like he's finally taking *me* seriously as well, instead of treating me like some "sweet" delusional girl.

I am also surprised by the new side of Aaron Davis I have been seeing. He's been alarmingly helpful with the party planning. Don't get me wrong, we're not becoming *friends* or anything, but maybe, just maybe, he's been downgraded from mortal enemy. Not that it's changed anything in the campaign department. . . I still plan to kick his butt, but at least he's starting to feel like a more worthy foe.

On the afternoon that the dance is taking place, Aaron and I meet to set things up. The rest of my team offered to help as well, but they've been working so hard that I really want them to just have a nice time. They're all coming to the dance later, and I want them to walk in and get the full effect. It is going to be brilliant.

"Oh. My. God," Aaron says when he walks in to the hall. His eyes widen and as I look around I realize that it is possible that I have gone a bit overboard. "Kostas," he whispers, shaking his head, "what have you done?"

"It's not my fault," I say quickly, pushing my way past the inflatable candy canes. "I got into some pretty tough negotiating with the party decoration people and about halfway into the second hour the guy cracked like a nut. He let me have everything for less than a quarter of the price." I gesture around me at the roomful of props and balloons. "All we have to do is make sure we put up the sign advertising 'Hank's Party Supplies', and mention their terrific prices over the loudspeaker."

"Oof." Aaron trips over a pile of plastic tubs. "What's this?" he asks.

"That's the liquid snow," I say. "For the snow machine."

My phone starts ringing. "Hang on, Aaron." I hold up one finger. "That'll be my reindeer guy." I make my way out of the hall to get better reception.

"Reindeer guy?" Aaron murmurs, gazing around him in bemusement. When I come back he's unpacking a box full of giant sparkly silver snowflakes that we're going to hang from the ceiling.

"This stuff is amazing," Aaron says grudgingly. "We never usually have anything like this. Are you sure you've done it on budget?"

I snort. As if I would ever exceed a budget. "I have

several spreadsheets and three graphs with the full breakdown on if you need to see them?" I say.

"No, no." Aaron shakes his head and holds his hands up in a gesture of surrender. "I believe you. I don't know how you managed it, but I believe you."

"So we'd better get started," I say then. "I mean, if we're going to get this finished in the next couple of hours, then we've got a ton of work to do."

Miss Sardana and Frank the caretaker arrive to help and then we're joined by a couple of the other teachers as well. Everyone seems slightly speechless when confronted with the decorations, and I am busy running around and shouting directions at people because for some reason they are finding it difficult to grasp my vision and I really want every detail to be perfect.

"Chill out, Kostas." Aaron grins at me over the shiny blue paper chains we are making. "This is going to be the best party Highworth Grange has ever seen. Just you wait."

I feel a shiver of anticipation running through me. I hope he's right.

By the time we finish setting up I don't have long to get home and get changed. Mum has come back early from the library so that she and Lil can help me get ready. After much deliberation we ordered a dress online that is made of silvery-blue material with long, floaty sleeves. It is silky and the material ripples between my fingers like water. Mum does my hair, carefully combing out all the tangles and smoothing the curls down. Lil lends me a lip balm that she bought with her pocket money that is peach and shimmery. When I'm ready I stand in front of them. "Well," I say, "what do you think?"

"Oh, Effie," Lil gasps. "You look just like Elsa." I know this is the highest compliment that she could possibly pay me. I actually do feel a bit like royalty this evening – you know, the kind of queen with brilliant superpowers who can create whole ice kingdoms and rule over her people with fairness and love.

"You look lovely." Mum smiles and looks a bit misty-eyed. "I hope you're going to enjoy yourself tonight ... I know you've been working so hard between catching up at school and running your campaign. We're all so proud of you."

The doorbell rings then, before it can get too emotional. "That will be Angelika!" I exclaim, and my teeth are practically chattering with excitement now. I bound down the stairs and fling the front door open. My best friend stands on the step, striking a pose. She is wrapped up in an enormous coat, a purple feather boa around her neck and silver glitter on her cheeks. Her eyes are sparkling, reflecting my own excitement back at me like a mirror, and we both squeal loudly for a minute or two while Dad stands in the background looking confused.

"Well, girls," he says finally, jangling his car keys in his hand. "Shall we go?"

CHAPTER *Twenty-Eight*

When we walk into the party it is like something out of a film. I hear Angelika gasp beside me and I feel a shiver of pride weaselling up and down my spine.

"OH. EM. GEE," Angelika mutters in hushed tones. "It's like being at the Oscars or something!"

As I look around at the sparkling, spangling, snow-filled scene in front of me I think she might have a point. There are giant silver snowflakes and pale blue streamers and paper chains hanging from the ceiling, twinkling in the light being thrown off an enormous glitter ball. In one corner a path of inflatable candy canes leads to a snowy enclosure where you can have your picture taken with Boris the reindeer. (Miss Sardana just stared, open-mouthed and speechless, when his owner, Toby, arrived in his little truck.) There are blue-and-silver tablecloths covering the long tables full of tasty party food, and big bunches of helium-filled balloons line the sides of the room. There's a long strip of pale blue carpet that leads to the dance floor, where quite a few of our fellow students are already pulling some impressive shapes in a cloud of dry ice.

Up on the stage there's a laptop connected to the big speakers that Aaron set up earlier, and he's made a massive playlist that should keep people dancing all night, or at least until 9.30 when the dance is due to finish and Toby needs to take Boris home for a nice bowl of whatever reindeer eat ... Weetabix or something probably. There's a LOT to take in, and it's definitely not the sort of spectacle that Highworth Grange will forget in a hurry.

"Hello, Effie." Miss Sardana appears at my side then.

"Hello, miss," I say, cheerfully. "It looks like it's all going well."

"It is. . ." Miss Sardana trails off here as though she can't quite find the words. "It is really something, Effie. I've never seen anything like it. You should be very proud. You and Aaron did a great job."

At the mention of his name I can't help but glance around to see if I can spot him.

"Come on, Effie." Angelika is tugging at my hand now. "I want to go and see the reindeer!"

As we make our way through the party I get stopped by quite a few people who want to talk about how good it all looks. Suddenly, the rest of the team appear.

"Effie! It's amazing!" Ruby yells over the music, her eyes shining. She's wearing a spangly gold jumpsuit and she looks stunning.

"It looks ace," Kevin says, straightening the stripy bow tie he is wearing.

"IS THAT A REINDEER?!" Jess thunders.

They are all looking brilliant and we hit the dance floor, laughing and joking, throwing ourselves around to the music. Even Zo is shuffling from side to side with a small smile on her lips. Kevin and Ruby get into a dance-off, Jess pulls out a spectacular robot and me and Angelika have our arms around each other as we sing along until our voices are hoarse. I feel completely and utterly happy. When we first moved here I found it so hard to imagine a scene like this, but here I am, dancing in the middle of a circle of brilliant friends, friends who have believed in me and worked so hard to help me achieve my dream. A warm glow spreads through me, as if I'm spinning around in a microwave of emotion.

After about half an hour we take a breather to go and get a drink. My face is red and giving off enough heat to act as a pretty decent radiator. I lift my heavy hair away from the back of my neck, welcoming the touch of cool air. My cheeks hurt from smiling so hard and my voice is gravelly as I yell to Angelika over the noise that I'm going to go to the toilets.

I start pushing my way through the crowds, and then I spot Aaron for the first time. He is wearing jeans and a dark blue shirt and he's standing in the middle of a big group of his friends. Matt Spader is there, wearing an almost identical outfit to Aaron, his gold hair shining under the disco lights. One of Aaron's arms is slung casually around Katie's shoulder. She looks gorgeous in a short, bright red dress, and I feel a little pang. Just then Aaron's eyes meet mine. I feel an unstoppable grin appear on my face and I lift my hand in a little wave.

An answering grin appears on Aaron's face, and he lifts the hand not currently around Katie's shoulder to give me a little salute. It's funny, but I know what he's thinking as clearly as if he'd just whispered it in my ear. *We did it!* I nod and smile again, because, really, we have pulled it off in epic style, and then I turn and carry on my way.

The girls' toilets are empty and I go over to the mirror. My reflection is pink and happy. My hair has grown dramatically in circumference thanks to the heat and I try to smooth it down with my fingers. I reach into the little sparkly bag that Mum lent me for Lil's lip balm and I put some more on, feeling quite grown-up to be the sort of girl who touches up her make-up at parties.

The door swings open then, banging against the wall with a thud that makes me jump.

"Oh, hi, Katie!" I exclaim, sunnily. "You gave me a bit of a shock!"

Katie's smile is bright and a bit tight, as if someone is pulling the corners up with invisible threads. "Hello, Effie," she says. "Good job on the party."

"Thanks," I reply, "but it wasn't all me," I add, fairly. "Aaron did a lot too."

"Yeah." Katie nods, coming to stand next to me and looking at her own reflection. She smooths her already perfect, silky hair. "Aaron said it was a bit of a drag, all that work. It's so boring for you that you both had to get roped into it."

I feel myself deflate a bit at that. I actually quite enjoyed the organizing process in the end, I hadn't realized Aaron found it such a chore. "Well, I guess Miss Sardana thought it was a good idea." I shrug. "You know, to help us get on a bit better."

"Mmm," Katie murmurs, still checking her face in the mirror. "It's a shame about that. I guess some people just can't get on with each other, it's nobody's fault, really."

"Oh, well, I . . ." I begin.

"I've told Aaron I think he's being a bit mean to you, but you know what boys are like." She sighs, and then her eyes meet mine in the mirror. "He was telling everyone it's been a bit embarrassing working together when you obviously fancy him so much. I mean, not that I can blame you!" Katie gives a tinkly little laugh at this. "But yeah, I guess it made him a bit uncomfortable and that's why he was saying all those things about you."

"What . . . what things?" I hear my voice ask from somewhere far away.

"You know, about how he feels sorry for you, and how you and your friends are all a bit weird. And how it's funny how seriously you're taking this whole thing, like it really matters." Katie shrugs. "I mean,

I guess it's not really fair that he doesn't have to try very hard to win, but people really like him, you know, they don't laugh at him. Not like. . ." She trails off here awkwardly, and lifts a hand to her mouth. "Oh, sorry," she says, "that came out a bit wrong."

I can feel my heart thundering in my chest. It's thumping so hard I'm a bit surprised that it doesn't bounce right out of my chest. "Oh, right," I say, and my voice is little more than a whisper.

"See you later, then," Katie sings, and she sashays back out the door.

I look in the mirror and the pink-cheeked, sparkly girl who was there before is gone. The face staring back at me now is pale and sad. I bite my lip, tasting the peachy lip balm, and give my reflection a stern order not to cry. Especially not over an idiot like Aaron Davis, a boy I don't even *like*. I grit my teeth and straighten my shoulders, and then I sweep majestically through the door, headed back to the party full of dignity and fierce feminist energy and only sniffling a very tiny bit.

Almost immediately, I spot Aaron and Katie. She is whispering in his ear and she turns to look at me and he is laughing. She's probably telling him about our conversation. I feel something burning and sad and hurt and angry rising up inside me. Then I hear someone calling my name. Dimly, I look around and realize that the voice is very loud and it's coming through the speakers. The music has stopped and people are turning in my direction. It's Miss Sardana's voice, and she's calling me and Aaron to the stage. I start making my way there, picking through the crowd just behind Aaron.

The party is finishing now and Miss Sardana is congratulating us on our hard work and people are applauding. Aaron is smiling like he hasn't got a care in the world, but I don't know what my face is doing. . . If how I feel is anything to go by, it's probably looking like the face of someone who wants to give another someone a reeeeealllly good telling off. Miss Sardana hands the microphone to Aaron.

"Thanks, miss," he says. "Hi, everyone!" The crowd goes wild. "Er, I guess I just wanted to say thanks for coming. Hope you have a good time!" He turns to me. "Effie, did you want to say something?" He holds out the microphone towards me. I know that I should take it and say something stirring, that I should show myself and the world that Aaron Davis feeling sorry for me or telling people that he thinks

I'm weird doesn't bother me one tiny little bit, but even as I try to tell myself that, I can feel something tightening in my chest, I can feel the tears prickling behind my eyes, and this time I think they're going to fall whether I like it or not.

"Kostas?" Aaron says.

I turn and run off the stage.

PART THREE

The Election

CHAPTER *Twenty-Nine*

My friends follow after me outside and I tell them that I'm not feeling very well. I am already kicking myself because I could have used that opportunity to make a stirring speech that would have swung loads of votes for me. Instead, I let myself be distracted by a few mean words. In the end Angelika gets the truth out of me and my campaign team are indignant.

"That Aaron Davis is the WORST," Jess says.

"Yeah, and he has absolutely no sense of style," Kevin puts in.

"He needs to pay." Ruby cracks her knuckles.

Zo tucks her arm through mine.

"Don't worry, Effie," Angelika says firmly. "None

of us cares what he thinks about us. We'll have the last laugh when you bring him down."

I smile a watery smile, touched by their support but feeling like the pressure to beat Aaron just keeps growing. I think about all the weeks that we've been working hard, campaigning with my team, and I wonder if I've done enough. My stomach is home to an entire family of butterflies.

I spend most of the weekend feeling a bit sorry for myself. Me, Mum and Lil have a duvet day on Saturday and Dad is on hand to supply hot chocolate and sweets. I don't tell them what had happened, but it is fairly obvious from my mood that things at the dance did not exactly go as planned.

"Why don't you choose the film?" Lil asks, dunking a fizzy red lace into her hot chocolate and slurping it up like spaghetti.

"What's the point of anything?" I groan, stuffing my head under a pillow and feeling rather than seeing a look pass between her and Mum.

"Look, Effie," Mum's voice croons, "Dad's put little marshmallows in your hot chocolate, just like you like. . ." The chocolatey steam reaches my face as she waves it gently beside the pillow like some delicious smelling salts.

"We could watch *Mulan*," Lil's voice sings persuasively. "You know an inspirational montage always cheers you up."

And it does actually cheer me up a bit, especially when the three of us jump to our feet, singing "I'll Make a Man Out of You" with such ferocity and realism that Dad comes running in to see what is wrong after Lil enthusiastically karate kicks a footstool.

Sunday is the day before the big debate and I go over all my notes again and again. I have to make sure that I am going to be ready, that there is no question that could possibly trip me up. There's no way I'm going to let Aaron get the better of me now. I work on my speech a lot, repeating it over and over again, until Mum, Dad and Lil are word perfect too.

"If you make me listen to that one more time..." Lil threatens across the dinner table, "I'll have my vengeance upon you."

"Oooh," I laugh. "What kind of vengeance?"

"The kind you won't see coming." Lil calmly picks up her dinner knife, and I decide to take the hint.

Back in school on Monday and it's the day of the big debate. It's the last chance we will have to convince voters that we're the right choice before the election tomorrow. It's strange, but the actual voting part seems to have crept up on me. I suppose that because I've been so busy and my head's been so full of the dance I haven't had so much time to think about it. Well, that's all over now and to be honest I'm finding it hard to think about anything else.

I am standing outside the school hall with my friends, getting ready to go in and face the music.

"Do you need a wee?" Jess asks, eyeing me uncertainly.

I suppose I am wiggling about rather a lot, but it feels like all my limbs have been taken over by jittery snakes. Maybe I shouldn't have had that cup of coffee with the vanilla syrup and squirty cream, but it seemed like a good idea at the time.

I try to picture how well the debate is going to go. I imagine climbing on to the stage, standing behind a golden podium. I see myself making a speech so powerful that my fellow students are overcome with emotion, openly weeping tears of joy and gratitude. I see Aaron, incapable of making any response, only saying, "I agree with Effie," in a broken voice, a single tear trickling down his cheek. I smile modestly and wave as the crowd leap to their feet, chanting my name. *Effie! Effie!*

"Effie!" Angelika's voice cracks my daydream open like a broken egg.

"Oh, sorry," I mumble. "What were you saying?"

"I was saying that it's time to go in." Angelika's eyes widen and she puffs out her cheeks before letting out a long breath. "Are you ready?"

I swallow hard, and my knees feel a bit trembly. "Born ready!" I boom, giving her a confident wink and a snappy click of my fingers.

Angelika looks mildly horrified. "Maybe don't do that again?" she suggests.

"Yeah," I agree. "I think you might be right."

She squeezes my arm and we file into the hall behind the others. The hall looks a bit different from the last time I was in here, and I think with a twinge of sadness about the winter wonderland that Aaron and I created. While the others all take their seats I make my way up to the stage on increasingly shaky legs. Unfortunately, there are no podiums at all (golden or otherwise) just a couple of plastic chairs pulled to one side of the stage.

Aaron Davis is already sprawled in one of the chairs, his long legs sticking out in front of him, his trademark glossy hair shining under the lights.

"All right, Kostas," he says in a way that I might

once have thought was friendly, but which I now see for the pitying sham that it is. Thanks to Katie, my eyes have been well and truly opened, and in my mind I see the two of them at the party, laughing together at how delusional I've been.

I don't even dignify him with an answer, sticking my nose up in the air and sweeping into the other seat, inching it as far away from him as possible.

Aaron looks a bit annoyed at being ignored. *Good*, I think fiercely, and before he can say anything else, Ms Shaarawi appears onstage, clapping her hands for silence.

"OK, everyone, thank you for coming in so quietly. It's an exciting day today as we have the junior class student council debate ahead of tomorrow's election. We haven't held the debate for several years so I'm very pleased to welcome you all here today." She turns to smile at me and Aaron. "This year we have two candidates running for junior class president, both excellent students, and I'm sure that whoever wins will do a wonderful job." Then Ms Shaarawi gets down to business. "So," she says. "We're doing things a little differently this year and I think we're in for a very interesting session. We'll be having a few minutes of debate on a range of different questions, and then each candidate will have ten minutes to speak. If I could ask Effie and Aaron to please come and stand up here." She stands aside and gestures to the front of the stage.

I take a deep breath and move into position. I've never noticed it before but this hall is humongous. It seems as if there are thousands and thousands of students stretching out in front of me in endless rows. And all of them are looking at me. Judging me. Waiting to hear what I have to say. I take a deep steadying breath. It doesn't matter how confident you are, or how much you know that you want to be prime minister, I guess standing up in front of a big group of people is always going to be a little nerve-racking. I hope for the sake of my political career that you get used to it with practice.

A hush fills the room.

My heart is pounding. There's no going back now.

"OK," Ms Shaarawi says, in a very official-sounding voice. "Let's begin with the first question."

CHAPTER *Thirty*

"What do you think is the most important responsibility for the junior class president?" Ms Shaarawi asks. "Effie, would you like to go first?"

"Yes," I squeak, "thank you, miss," I finish, lowering my voice to a pitch that humans can hear. I pause for a second to gather my thoughts. "I think that a good president has a responsibility to his or her fellow students to try and make the school the best place it can possibly be for everyone. Whether that's through improving facilities, or supporting more clubs and societies, or concentrating on student safety, or making sure that there is help for students who are being bullied... I think the most important thing is to keep coming up with new ideas, to have imagination and to be good at solving problems."

"Thank you, Effie." Ms Shaarawi smiles, and the room fills with polite applause. I look down at the front row, where my team have positioned themselves, and they all give me little thumbs-up signals. "Now, Aaron, over to you."

Aaron smiles winningly and looks thoughtful. I realize I am holding my breath. "I think Effie's point is interesting," Aaron say finally, "but I think for me the most important responsibility is to make sure everything keeps running smoothly. I think it's important to do new things, but you don't want to overload yourself or stretch the student council too thin. I think our school is great, and even though I agree that we could make some changes for the better, I think that those should be decided by the students. I know, for example, that a lot of people want to see changes in the school dinner menu. That's the sort of small, practical thing that the student council president can achieve."

I can feel my mouth clunk open as a hearty round of applause sweeps through the room. "WOOO!" I hear one person yell. "PIZZZZAAAAAA!"

"But don't you think there are more important issues than pizza?" I ask.

Aaron shrugs. "I think if pizza is important to my fellow students, then it is important to me." Another, smaller round of whoops fills the air here.

"OK," Ms Shaarawi interrupts here. "That's very interesting; let's move on to the next question."

The questions continue and I think I'm doing a pretty good job of answering all of them. Unfortunately, so is Aaron. I might not agree with everything he says but, frustratingly, he's actually making some good points and it's clear that he's really thought about this. I'm especially impressed with his suggestion of a feedback box, where students can leave anonymous questions or concerns for the student council – a couple of weeks ago I would *never* have imagined these words coming out of Aaron Davis's mouth. I can feel my heart thumping as we argue over different issues, but it's a good kind of heart thumping ... like when you're playing a game that makes you feel nervous and excited at the same time and you're really concentrating on doing your best.

The whole time Aaron is making his speech I try really hard to focus but it's my own speech that I hear running around and around on a loop in my head. What I do hear is the cheer that he gets at the end. It lasts a long time. When it's my turn I get to my feet and move to the middle of the stage. There is a moment of silence, and it almost feels like I'm about to start twirling and singing in some big Broadway number. But now is not the time for daydreams, Effie!

I clear my throat. "My fellow students," I begin, "I am here today because I care about you. I care about every person in this room, and I care about the school that we are sitting in." I go on to outline several of my biggest plans – the green initiative to dramatically improve school recycling, the buddy system so that no one is left feeling alone or excluded from school life, the fundraising that I want to do for the library so that everyone has access to all the books that they want and to a librarian who can help them find the perfect book for them.

"Also, the student council is responsible for distributing the funds to clubs and societies," I say. "In the past I don't believe that this has been handled fairly. There are lots of clubs that don't get funding and in most cases don't even know that there is any money available. I would like to see the money divided more fairly so the art club can have a trip to a museum, and the creative writing club can have an author visit to the school. I want to make sure that the gamers and the gymnasts and the aspiring actors all get to have their own societies – fun, safe places for students to go and meet people who share their interests." There's a round of applause here, as if the room has perked up a bit.

"I know that I am new to this school," I say, finally. "I know that some of you don't know me very well, but it didn't take long for me to find a home here at Highworth Grange. It didn't take long for me to find people who challenge me, or a brilliant group of friends, who have supported me." I look at my team then, and I feel my chin wobble a bit at this. "When I started this campaign it was just me and a broom cupboard, but with the help of the amazing people sitting down there –" I gesture to my pals, who squirm in their seats "– it became something so much bigger. I've met lots of you now, and I've listened to you. I've shown that I can get things done, I've shown that I take this seriously. Some might say *too* seriously."

I pause here and carefully keep my eyes from travelling to where Aaron is sitting. "But let me tell you why I take it so seriously. It's because I think it's important. Sometimes, when you're a kid, but especially when you're a girl, people want you to be quiet and well-behaved. They don't want you to take up too much space. They don't want you getting too excited about changing things because they like the way things are. It's comfortable, and easy for them ... but changing things is important. Things shouldn't just stay the same; we should ask questions about what's right and how things could be better for everyone.

"Less than a hundred years ago women couldn't vote. Now I know that one day I could be the prime minister. That only happened because loads and loads of women made themselves bigger and noisier and didn't listen when other people told them they were taking things too seriously."

I pause again here, thinking about Iris and her box of newspaper clippings, of her saying that I had opportunities she could only dream of. For a second I let myself enjoy being up here onstage, I let myself enjoy being listened to and taken seriously. I think about all the girls and women who helped to make it possible by speaking up and making themselves heard. I take a deep breath. "So, I'm Effie Kostas, and yes, I'm loud, and yes, I make trouble, and yes, I want to change things, and yes, I take this seriously . . . but that's exactly why you should vote for me, because I don't just want my voice to be heard, I want *your* voice to be heard too. And I want to make sure that people are listening. Thank you."

There's a moment of silence, and I feel an overwhelming wave of panic rising inside me. Oh no. They hated it. I got it all wrong.

Then Angelika starts clapping, and Jess, and Ruby, and Kevin, and Zo. Then *everyone* is clapping and they're clapping so loudly that the sound is echoing off the walls. "WOOOO! EFFIE!" I hear a girl's voice cheer. I look over at the back of the room and there is Miss Sardana . . . and instead of her usual weary expression she is grinning and dabbing at her eyes. I feel a rush of joy surge through me that leaves me buzzing like I've drunk a hundred cups of coffee. The clapping goes on and on, getting louder. It must be as loud as it was for Aaron, I think, it's definitely close.

"Well, thank you all," Ms Shaarawi says now, coming to the middle of the stage. "And a very big thank-you to both of our candidates. I have to say that I am so glad that we have had this debate today because it raised a lot of important and interesting issues. This year's campaign has been very different from the others during my time here, and I am so thrilled to see such switched-on and engaged students. You make me hopeful for the future of our school and you should both be extremely proud of yourselves, whatever the outcome is." She smiles at me and at Aaron, who has come to stand beside me. "Voting will take place tomorrow during your morning registration, and we'll announce the new student council at the end of the day."

Ms Shaarawi directs everyone to leave and chatter fills the air as everyone begins filing out. I am still trembling with excitement and adrenaline as I go to collect my bag from beside my chair.

"Hey, great job, Kostas." I hear a voice beside me, and I turn to find Aaron grinning at me. "That speech was really good."

"Thanks," I say frostily. "I guess I should thank you for the inspiration."

"Yeah," Aaron says ruefully, rubbing his neck, "I suppose at the beginning. . ."

"You don't need to pretend any more." I cut him off here. "I know what you think about me, what you've been saying about me and I *so* don't care."

"What are you talking about?" Aaron looks confused.

"Feeling sorry for me, laughing at me, making fun of me and my friends." I point at him. "I heard all about it, and let me tell you, my friends are worth a MILLION of you."

Aaron's cheeks are turning red and he stares at me wordlessly.

"And I don't know how many times I have to say it before it makes its way into your thick head, but I don't LIKE you like that. OK? I don't like you AT ALL." My voice is an angry growl by the end.

Aaron's own face is getting pretty angry now as well. "Well, don't worry," he snaps, picking up his own school bag. "You don't have to say it again. Message received. And maybe next time you should check your facts before you pick a fight with someone." And with that he stalks off.

I should feel victorious. I should feel good about telling him off. Instead, as I stand on the empty stage in the empty hall, I just feel confused and uncertain.

CHAPTER *Thirty-One*

"Election day!" a voice shouts. "ELECTION DAY ELECTION DAY ELECTION DAY!" The voice is accompanied by some serious banging sounds.

I open my eyes blearily, just in time to see Lil burst through my bedroom door, bashing two pan lids together like cymbals. "ELECTION DAAAAAAAAAY!" she screeches.

I leap out of bed. "Yeah, all right, thanks, Lil. . ." I croak. "I was hardly likely to forget." It took me a long time to get to sleep last night and my eyes feel all small and gluey. I yawn a massive yawn – one that leaves me swaying on my feet.

"I brought you the glittery hair scrunchie of DESTINY!" Lil cries dramatically, dropping the pan lids with a crash and reaching into her pocket to pull out a very purple, very glittery scrunchie, which she brandishes in the air like Rafiki holding Simba in *The Lion King*. "It's for luck," she adds.

"Thank you," I say, touched by my sister's thoughtfulness. Even though it is sparkly and ridiculous I slip the scrunchie on to my wrist, and I do think I feel a teeny tiny bit braver.

"So, when you're president," Lil says, "will I get special privileges? Will I be like the Presidential Sister? Do I get a title? I was thinking *Empress of State* has a nice ring to it. . ."

"You don't get anything," I mumble, "and I haven't won yet." I think back to yesterday's debate. It went well, but did it go well enough? People really seemed to enjoy my speech, but the cheering was just as loud for Aaron . . . maybe even a little bit louder. I suppose I have to admit that he did an all right-ish job in the end. Even if he was just playing up to the crowd.

My insides feel all jumbled up, as if they are swirling around in a washing machine. I want to win so badly – there are people counting on me. What if I let them down? I try to push the feelings aside, but they are too big and too noisy to ignore.

When I get downstairs, Dad has made banana pancakes and he seems even more nervous than me.

"I just want you to *know*," he insists, "that win or lose, we're all so proud of you for doing this."

"I *do* know, Dad," I say, trying to remain patient. "You've told me four times since I sat down for breakfast. You and Mum both told me last night. It's written in the good-luck card you slipped under the door. You wrote PROUD OF YOU in chocolate chips on my pancakes. Honestly, I get it."

"It's just..." Dad is starting to get choked up now, and Lil and I share a slightly panicked look. He's so soppy once he gets going.

"I hope he's not going to start talking about when they brought you back from the hospital," Lil whispers to me.

"When I think about the day we brought you back from the hospital..." Dad sniffles and Lil's head hits the table. "You were so tiny..."

"OK, Dad," I sing. "Got to go now! Love you!"

"Love ... you ... too..." Dad chokes as I speed away and out of the front door, as I glance over my shoulder I see Lil standing next to him, a pained expression on her face.

"There, there," she says, patting Dad gingerly on

the arm as he sniffles into a piece of kitchen towel. "It's not as bad as when you had to leave me for my first day of primary school, is it?"

"Oooooh!" Dad howls.

I beat a hasty retreat.

Outside the school gates I find the whole team waiting for me.

"So, today's the day!" Angelika says brightly, slipping her arm through mine.

They all look almost as nervous as I feel. There's a big lump in my throat as I look at them. We've worked so hard, and this whole thing is about all of us. It might be my name on the ballot but if I lose I'm going to have let them all down. I can hardly bear to think about it.

"Well, at least I know I'll be getting six votes." I smile weakly at them.

"I don't know." Kevin taps his chin. "I did like what Aaron had to say about the pizza..." Ruby wallops him on the arm. "Joking, joking!" he says quickly.

"Listen," I say, taking a deep breath. "I just need you guys to know that whatever happens, working with you has been the best thing about this whole election. I couldn't have done it without you."

We all huddle into a sort of group hug then.

The bell rings with a shrill *Brrrrrrrrrrrrr!* And I shiver. It's time for morning registration, and that means time for everyone to cast their votes. I feel a wave of panic washing over me at the thought of it.

"Come on then," Jess says. "Let's go and vote for Effie."

We all follow her inside.

The day drags out as slowly as you would expect. I think my lessons are going to go on and on for ever and ever. It's like time has slowed down, like my teachers are talking in slow motion. I'm so nervous and wound up that by the time the bell finally goes late in the afternoon to tell us it's time for the special assembly where the announcements will be made, I think I might throw up or faint, or throw up THEN faint.

When I get up to the stage again Aaron is already waiting there. Even he looks nervous; his mouth is in a thin straight line as he fiddles with his tie.

"Davis," I say briskly.

"Kostas," he replies, not meeting my eye.

"Hello, everybody!" I jump as Ms Shaarawi arrives on the stage. "I don't want to keep everyone in

suspense for too long, so I will just get on with it."
I breathe a sigh of relief here. "So, the results are in,
and we'll begin with junior student secretary." Ms
Shaarawi looks down at the piece of paper in her
hand. "And the winner is, Angelika Lisowski!" I clap
so hard that my hands hurt and cheer as loudly as I
can. Even though Angelika was the only one to run I
think that's partly because everyone knew she would
be the best person for the job. Angelika stands up
from her seat and takes a bow and we share a grin.
I'm so pleased for her, but now it seems as though
the butterflies in my stomach are flapping up a real
storm. Angelika's in again, but what about me?

Ms Shaarawi announces the role of treasurer next,
a girl I don't know called Charlotte. I think Luna
looks relieved . . . she's pretty busy with all her other
societies.

Finally, finally it's time to announce the winner
of junior class president. Aaron and I stand side by
side. I look out into the audience and catch Angelika's
eye. "GOOD LUCK," she mouths. I nod. My knees
are shaking so hard it's taking pretty much all my
concentration just to make sure I don't fall over.

"And this year the competition between our two
candidates for president has been really tight," Ms

Shaarawi says. "In fact, there were fewer than twenty votes between them." I feel my heart squeeze at this. "And before I announce the winner, I just think we should have a round of applause for Effie and Aaron, who have both worked very hard." I smile grimly as everyone applauds politely. I wish she'd get on with it.

"So without further ado," Ms Shaarawi says, "the junior class president this year is..." There's a pause where the room goes so quiet you could hear a feather drop, never mind a pin.

It seems to go on for ever and ever.

I find myself wondering how old I am now.

Am I an old lady?

This pause has been going on for so long that my life seems to pass before me. Soon I'll be just a pile of dust on this stage and people will sing folk songs about it.

Ms Shaarawi clears her throat and it seems our wait might be over.

"... Aaron Davis!" she exclaims.

Whoosh! I feel all the air leave my body.

I lost, I think numbly.

I really lost.

I try and make sense of how I'm feeling; I try and

come up with any other thoughts, but it's as though those two words are the only thing left in my brain, written in huge black letters.

I. Lost.

I close my eyes briefly, as the cheers for Aaron fill my ears. I plaster on a wobbly smile and turn to face him. He looks as shocked as I feel. I hold out my hand and he takes it, wrapping his fingers around mine. We shake solemnly.

"Congratulations," I choke out.

"Thank you," he says, dazed. "I thought it would be you."

I don't know what to say to that so I just shrug awkwardly. "You did really well," I say.

"So did you," Aaron replies, and I think he means it. Not that it's much comfort at the moment.

"OK, well, congratulations to our new student council," Ms Shaarawi says, "and can we have another round of applause for everyone."

I can't look at the audience; I can't bear to see my friends. I can't bear to see the pity on all those faces. As soon as I can, I drift off the stage in a complete stupor and rush through the corridors. I don't even know exactly where I'm headed until I arrive outside the cupboard door. I yank it open and disappear inside.

I don't turn the light on, preferring to hide here in the darkness for a while.

I sit on one of the cushions with my knees pulled up to my chest. I don't know how long I sit there in silence. Finally, there's a light tap on the door, and someone pushes it open. It's Zo. I can see the silhouette of her coat in the doorway.

"Hi, Zo," I sniffle.

Zo closes the door behind her and comes to sit beside me in the dark. Her silent presence is comforting. We sit for a minute in the quiet; the only sound is me sniffing sadly.

Then a small voice breaks the silence. "Are you OK?" Zo asks. Her voice is low and a little croaky and I am so surprised

to hear it that it shocks me out of my tears. I can feel Zo's arm on my shoulder and my body sags into hers.

"Not really," I admit, finally.

There's more silence then. Perhaps that's the end of the conversation. After all, those three words are the first I have heard Zo speak at all. It means a lot that she used her voice to help me feel less alone.

"I think you were brilliant." Zo's voice wavers in the darkness then. "Doing what you did. It was so brave. I couldn't have been so brave."

"Oh, well. . ." I say awkwardly, my heart bumping slightly.

"No," Zo interrupts, firmly. "I couldn't. Before you decided to run, before I joined your team, I was too scared to do anything. Not just talk." She gives a little chuckle here. "I know I still don't do much of that. But I could hardly stand to come into school. Since I've been part of this group I've been to school every day," Zo continues. "I went to a *dance*," she marvels. "I have *friends*. I didn't think that would happen." There's a little pause. "I was bullied at my last school. It was . . . really bad. In the end I just refused to go, and my mum moved me here. I couldn't talk to anyone. I couldn't join in. I thought if I tried then it would all start again." There's another pause and I hold my breath. I can't believe Zo is sharing all of this with me. It's as if every word is an effort, being pulled out of her, and I don't want to interrupt.

"When I heard about you, and when I saw your poster, I knew that you had been on your own as well. I saw you at lunchtimes, sitting by yourself, but you didn't see me. I used to just get my lunch and then go and eat in the toilets. But I thought maybe . . . maybe we could be friends. I loved working with you and I believe in you, in all the things you're going to do." Zo shuffles in her seat. "When you talked about setting up the mentoring campaign, and about making sure that no one had to eat their lunch by themselves, I felt like finally someone had seen me. What you're doing is important. You can't stop now. Not just because you lost a stupid election. I won't let you." With that Zo lets out a long, shuddering breath.

I'm kind of glad she can't see the tears running down my cheeks. I reach out and throw my arms around her. "Thanks, Zo," I mutter into her shoulder. "Thank you so much. I — I really needed that."

"That's all right." Zo laughs again into the darkness. We sit quietly for another moment and even though I'm still sad, it feels as if Zo's words were a little sliver of light breaking through the clouds. If the campaign made a difference to even one person then it must all have been worth it. At least, that's what I'm going to keep telling myself until I believe it.

CHAPTER *Thirty-Two*

"Oh, it's you," Iris greets me a little later. "Come in then, you're letting all the cold air in." She has already turned away from the door and is hobbling back inside. When we get to the kitchen, Lennon is getting some exercise and he flies around the room before settling on Iris's shoulder, where he headbutts her affectionately.

"SILLY OLD BAG!" Lennon croaks at his most loving.

"Who are you calling old?" Iris grumbles, bustling about making cups of tea. I notice that her hair has been freshly dyed and is the same vibrant hot pink as her kitchen walls. Long strands of beads click and clack around her neck as she moves. "So today was the big vote, eh?" She settles a steaming mug in front of me and I wrap my fingers around the warm china.

"Yep." I nod.

"Well?" Iris raises an eyebrow. "How did it go?"

"It went badly," I reply, my voice flat and low. "I lost."

Iris doesn't say anything, and I feel a tear snake down my cheek.

There's a slight scraping noise and I look down to see her slowly pushing a dish of biscuits across the table towards me.

I reach out and take one, dunking it carefully in my tea. It helps a bit.

"Sorry," I sniffle. "I'm still a bit upset about it."

"Don't apologize for having feelings," Iris says. "You should be proud of what you achieved. I bet a lot of people voted for you."

"Well, yes, I suppose," I admit. "Our head teacher did say that there were less than twenty votes between us."

"And how many junior students are there?" Iris asks.

"In all three years?" I say thoughtfully, doing the maths in my head. "About five hundred."

Iris sips her tea. "So over two hundred people who believed in you and voted for you?" She raises her eyebrows. "That's no small thing."

"No," I say, dazed. "It's not, is it?"

We sit quietly for a moment while I think this over.

"Aaron actually did a surprisingly good job," I admit, staring into my cup of tea. "Even if he totally played up to the crowd."

"Hmm," Iris says again. "Well, from what you've told me about him, that's a bit of a surprise."

I frown. "I suppose he's not as bad as I first thought ... at the school council thing, anyway. As a human being he pretty much sucks."

We sit in silence for a minute and I can practically feel all the events of the day whirring around and around in my head like a demented carousel.

"We had a fight," I say, finally.

"Who did?" Iris asks.

"Me and Aaron. We had a fight because I heard he was saying mean things about me and my friends." I sigh. "The thing is —" I pick at my fingernails "— I thought we were ... well ... I had almost started to think we might be ... *friends*."

Iris slurps her tea some more. "And this fight," she

says, "did you give him a chance to share his side?"

"What side?" I snort.

"You and me are quite a lot alike, Effie Kostas," Iris says gruffly. "Always charging into battle. Now I'm not saying the boy isn't an idiot . . . maybe he is. But if you thought the two of you were friends then maybe you should trust your judgement a bit more. Give him the benefit of the doubt."

I think about this carefully. "Hmmm, maybe," I say finally, although I'm not convinced.

"Anyway." Iris's gaze sharpens as it rests on me. "The point is, if you did your best, then win or lose, you should be proud of yourself." Her voice is brisk.

I snort again. "That sounds like the sort of thing you say to a real loser."

Iris lifts a finger warningly. "Now you listen to me, Effie Kostas," she says. "If you had lost this election spectacularly, if you hadn't even got a single vote, if your loss was so enormous and embarrassing—"

"Yeah, all right," I interrupt in alarm. "I get the picture."

"EVEN then," Iris continues as though I haven't spoken, "no one could ever think of you as a loser."

It's so unexpectedly sweet that I feel my eyes tingling with tears. It's been a strange day and I'm feeling so overwhelmed – sad and hurt and angry at the same time.

"What you've done, Effie," Iris continues solemnly, "is very brave. You didn't let being new or being scared stop you from running. You didn't stay quiet. You made sure people heard you. And they listened." Her hand reaches out and squeezes mine. Her skin is papery thin, but her grip is firm and I squeeze back, gratefully. We sit like that for a couple of seconds and then she snatches her fingers away and looks at me suspiciously, as if I've somehow tricked her into being nice to me. "Now," she huffs, "if you've quite finished feeling sorry for yourself then you can help me with this Netflix thing that your sister has talked me into getting. Looks like a lot of rubbish to me." She sniffs derisively. "Probably full of soap operas and young people nonsense." Her tone might be dismissive but her eyes gleam with excitement at the prospect and I can tell she's going to be knee-deep in *The Vampire Diaries* before long.

"No problem," I smile. "I can help with that."

Later that evening I'm snuggled up under a blanket eating a huge plate of chocolate brownies. It wasn't quite as bad as I thought it would be, telling my family that I had lost. They wanted me to know they were really proud of me A LOT, and Dad put on a T-shirt that said PROUD DAD on the front, just in case I wasn't totally convinced. Lil brooded for quite a while and began asking really specific questions about Aaron's timetable and his route home from school until I told her it wasn't Aaron's fault, not really.

"I still can't BELIEVE I was going to let him duet with me," she muttered darkly, and then, as if struck by a sudden thought, "HE'S LIKE A REAL-LIFE HANS!"

It's dark outside now and there's a knock at the door. "Effie," I hear Dad call. "It's someone for you."

Weird.

I stagger to my feet, brushing the chocolate crumbs from my clothes and smoothing my tangled hair.

Standing in the doorway is Aaron Davis.

"What are you doing here?" I blurt out.

He looks down at the ground, scuffing his toes on the front doorstep.

"I don't really know," he says, and his voice is quiet. "I just wanted to say ... you know ... good campaign or whatever."

I look at him for a moment. His cheeks are a bit

pink and I realize it can't have been easy to come here.

"I'm sorry about yesterday," I say, taking a deep breath. Because Iris is right. I should give him the benefit of the doubt. I don't much feel like I need a mortal enemy any more. "I shouldn't have snapped at you without giving you a chance to share your side of the story," I offer.

Aaron looks up. "I honestly don't know what you heard," he says quickly. "But it's not true. I never made fun of you or your friends. I know we didn't get on at the beginning, and I know I said some stupid things but I thought we were. . ." He shrugs helplessly. "You know . . . all right now."

"We are all right." I smile weakly. "I guess we both said things. It doesn't really matter."

"Cool," Aaron says, shuffling his feet.

"Cool," I echo. "So, anyway ... congratulations and all that."

"Oh. Thanks," Aaron says awkwardly. Then he seems to take a deep breath. "Look, the real reason I came was to say that you were right. About me. About a lot of things."

My mouth drops open. These are the last words I expected to hear. "I'm sorry," I say. "Could you repeat that?"

Aaron gives me a lopsided grin. "I couldn't stop thinking about what you said about the girls' football team —" his voice is very serious "– about doing things that help other people, not just doing things for yourself. I hadn't really thought about that before." He shakes his head. "Not like I had consciously been ignoring things I could be doing as student president, exactly ... more like I just hadn't thought about them." He frowns. "Does that make sense?"

"Sort of," I say.

"Anyway –" he shrugs "– I just wanted you to know that I want to try and do things differently now. Probably not exactly how you would do them, but I want to ... do more. Thanks to you."

I let out a long breath. "That's ... good," I say.

"Yeah." He shrugs again, not quite meeting my eye.

"Especially because I'm going to be around to make sure you keep all your promises," I say, my hand on my hip as I feel something big and hopeful filling my chest. "And if you let the students down then I'll be the one leading the resistance."

Aaron grins now, and I can feel my face grinning back at him.

He turns to walk back up the garden path. "We'll

see, Kostas," he calls over his shoulder.

"We *will* see, Davis!" I yell after him. "And the first thing I'm coming for is your lunch pass!"

He raises his hand in a jaunty salute and I close the door, leaning back against it. I can hear Iris and Zo's words ringing in my ears. My job here is far from done.

In fact, I'm just getting started.

Epilogue

"Come on, Effie, you can do better than that," Iris snaps as I push her wheelchair through the crowd. "Let's get over there!"

"I'm trying!" I wheeze.

"Here, let me," Jess says. "It's my turn."

I move aside gladly, and Jess proves more nimble with the wheelchair than me, guiding us over to one side.

"WOOOOO!" Iris cries, waving her sign in the air with both hands. The sign reads: I'M NINETY YEARS OLD AND I CAN'T BELIEVE I STILL HAVE TO PROTEST THIS STUFF. Around us a group of women cheer and laugh. A couple ask if they can take a picture of her and Iris cackles gleefully.

"Of course you can," she says, obviously very pleased with herself.

Lil, dressed as Princess Leia, is getting almost as much attention. She's holding tightly on to Dad's hand, but in her other hand is a sign that says A GIRL'S PLACE IS IN THE RESISTANCE. We made it together, breaking out all the glitter glue.

"This is the coolest thing I've ever done," Angelika says, slipping her arm through mine and grinning at me.

She's so completely right. We are standing in a crowd of thousands of people, marching through the streets of London for women's rights and equality. There are people here from all over. They are every age, every race, from everywhere, and they are singing and chanting and walking together.

"You dropped your glove," a voice says from beside me.

"Thanks." I smile, reaching out to take it.

"No worries," Aaron replies, returning my smile. "Thanks for bringing me today," he says, looking

around him. "This is awesome."

"I'm glad you came," I say. And I realize that I really am.

I remember what Iris told me once, about feeling part of something bigger than yourself. Of feeling like you were in the middle of something important. That's how I feel now. It's a feeling that is so big it seems almost impossible to keep it inside, and so I shout and sing along as loud as I can. I look around at my friends, who have all come to march. They're waving signs and laughing together. I know I'm so lucky to have them, and that they help me feel part of something too.

"SHOUT UP, SHOUT OUT, SHOUT LOUD!" the crowd chant. "TOGETHER WE WILL CHANGE THE WORLD!"

I really couldn't agree more.

READING *Questions:*

I hope that you enjoyed reading Effie's story as much as I enjoyed writing it. Effie loves having conversations with people and asking important questions, so I know she would be really happy if this book got readers talking. Hopefully you can come up with some questions of your own, but here are a few to get you started.

Effie campaigns for issues like recycling and libraries. Aaron campaigns for pizza. What issues would you campaign for in your school?
What would you like to see change?

Aaron and Effie argue throughout the book. Do you think they will ever be able to work together?

Aaron wins the presidential campaign. Do you think he has changed over the book? Will he be a different president now?

Have you ever lost a competition? How did you pick yourself up afterwards?

What are the qualities that make a good leader?

In the book Effie is often told that she's being too loud or too opinionated. What do you think about her response?

What job would you want on Effie's campaign team?

USEFUL *Links:*

If you're feeling inspired by Effie and her friends,
or if there were issues in the book that you want
to learn more about, then these are some different
websites that you might find interesting. There are
lots of ways that you can make a difference.

obama.org/globalgirlsalliance/

assembly.malala.org/

girlup.org/take-action/be-a-leader/girl-up-clubs/

amightygirl.com

girlguiding.org.uk/
social-action-advocacy-and-campaigns

womensmarchlondon.com/bring-the-noise

lettoysbetoys.org.uk/letbooksbebooks

thisgirlcan.co.uk

sciencegrrl.co.uk

pbskids.org/scigirls

engineergirl.org

banbossy.com

fawcettsociety.org.uk

stemettes.org

friendsoftheearth.uk

wastebuster.co.uk

bulliesout.com

youngminds.org.uk

Acknowledgements

I love this book a lot and it came about because of a conversation with my agent Louise Lamont and my editor Gen Herr about the amazing kids we were encountering, and the terrible sadness we felt about the state of the world, and what work we could make that was hopeful and honest in the face of these things. We worked together to come up with Effie Kostas and her friends and so the first thanks must go to them, my collaborators and my friends.

My incredible editor Sophie Cashell was Effie's number one cheerleader. She literally cut out yearbook photos of Amy Poehler and marched into acquisitions telling them why we needed to make this book. She waved banners, she bought cakes. Her notes were, as always, frustratingly spot on and her enthusiasm and sense of humour made working on this book such a joy. Thank you so much, Sophie!

To the rest of the team at Scholastic, I can't thank you enough for continuing to support me – I have always felt like I am in the safest possible hands with you. I still can't believe that I get to work with such an incredible, passionate, dedicated group of people. You have genuinely made my dreams come true!

To my friends and family who have been a constant source of love and support even when I have been moaning over deadlines and weeping over my computer screen. Thank you for putting up with me! Thank you to my niece Imogen and my nephew Alex for being my continuing source of inspiration. I am a very proud auntie thanks to these two incredible young people. Thank you to my lovely friend Lynda for lending me her parrot... I'm sorry I made him so badly behaved, the real Lennon is very polite! Special thanks, love, and lemon juice to my pal, Chris Yiannitsaros. And as always the biggest thank you to Paul for being my best friend and the very kindest person I know, and for blaming the patriarchy whenever necessary.

And thank you, thank you, thank you, to you. Thank you for reading and for caring. Thank you for being the person you are and for taking up space. Now, I hope you feel inspired and, as Effie would say, I hope you go out there and make some noise!

LAURA WOOD

Effie THE
REBEL

SHE'S SAVING   **THE WORLD**
ONE CLASSROOM AT A TIME